"What's Wrong, Call?"

Haven asked. "You seem…I don't know, angry, or frustrated, or…" She shook her head.

Tell her, Call's mind yelled. Tell her that Brian was a traitor to his country, and that fact was now possibly placing her and Paige in harm's way.

Tell her. Tell her that nothing, *nothing,* was going to happen to her or her baby. Anyone with an intention of hurting her would have to get past him, and that wasn't going to happen.

Tell her. Tell her that he had pulled the trigger on the gun that had killed Brian Larson.

Damn it, Call, tell her….

Dear Reader,

Just when you thought Mother Nature had turned up the heat, along comes Silhouette Desire to make things even *hotter*. It's June...the days are longer, the kids are out of school, and we've got the very best that romance has to offer.

Let's start with our *Man of the Month, Haven's Call,* which is by Robin Elliott, a writer many of you have written to tell me is one of your favorites.

Next, we have *Salty and Felicia* by Lass Small. If you've ever wondered how those two older Browns got together, well, now you'll get to find out! From Jennifer Greene comes the latest installment in her JOCK'S BOYS series, *Bewildered.* And Suzanne Simms's series, HAZARDS, INC., continues with *The Pirate Princess.*

Anne Marie Winston has created a tender, wonderful story, *Substitute Wife.* And if you like drama and intensity with your romance, don't miss Lucy Gordon's *Uncaged!*

It just doesn't get any better than this...so read and enjoy.

All the best,

Lucia Macro
Senior Editor

Please address questions and book requests to:
Reader Service
U.S.: P.O. Box 1325, Buffalo, NY 14269
Canadian: P.O. Box 1050, Niagara Falls, Ont. L2E 7G7

ROBIN ELLIOTT
HAVEN'S CALL

SILHOUETTE *Desire*®
Published by Silhouette Books
America's Publisher of Contemporary Romance

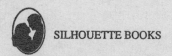 SILHOUETTE BOOKS

ISBN 0-373-05859-4

HAVEN'S CALL

ROBIN ELLIOTT

lives in a small, charming town in the high pine country of Arizona. She enjoys watching football, attending craft shows on the town square and gardening. Robin has published over sixty novels and also writes under her own name, Joan Elliott Pickart.

For my grandson,
Jeremiah Scott Kuntz,
and for
(in order of arrival)
Heather Marie, Jayce Tanner, Christopher David.

Miracles.
Welcome to the world!

One

Call Shannon slouched lower in the chair opposite the desk, fingers laced loosely on his chest. His Stetson was pulled low on his forehead, shadowing his face.

The short, round man sitting behind the large, highly polished mahogany desk was talking on the telephone, but Call tuned out what was being said. Barely moving his head, his gaze swept over the room, his mind cataloging all that he saw.

The office, which was on the twelfth floor of a modern high rise, was big and richly furnished, the earth-tone decor clearly announcing that the man in command wished no hint of feminine frills in his private domain.

Floor-to-ceiling windows made up one entire wall, providing a breathtaking view of the Houston skyline. The windows sparkled, with no speck of dust, soot or streak of past rain in evidence. It was as though even the birds knew that the one within that room would not tolerate any undesirable addition to what was his.

Along the inside walls, bookcases of gleaming mahogany rose from the floor to touch the ceiling, displaying a multitude of books bound in butter-soft leather. Intermixed among the volumes were rare artifacts from countries large and small around the world. Each token of a time past represented a memory, some welcome, others detested, of separate eras of a life not spent in idle wandering.

Peter MacIntosh, the man speaking on the telephone, was fifty-eight years old, and was dressed completely in white; suit, shirt, tie, socks, shoes—even the narrow ring of hair that remained on his nearly bald head was snowy white.

He replaced the receiver, then sniffed the air, his small twitching nose resembling that of a curious rabbit.

"I smell it, Call," Peter said. "I smell it. You actually came in here with horse dung on your boots. You've got a helluva nerve, do you know that?"

Call pushed up the sweat-stained Stetson with one thumb, and raised a dark eyebrow as he looked at the edge of the boot he had propped at the ankle on his other knee. He nodded slowly, a thoughtful expression on his tanned face.

"Yep," he said. His voice was deep, befitting a man who stood six-foot-three in his stocking feet. "That's horse dung, all right. But—" he shifted his gaze to the older man "—considering that you said it was an emergency, plus the fact that this office is about the last place on earth I'd choose to spend my time, you're lucky I didn't decide to scrape my boots clean on the edge of your fancy desk, MacIntosh. You know I'm not a happy man when I wear my working hat into town. This sweaty, dirty Stetson is definitely my working hat."

"No need to get so hostile, boy," Peter MacIntosh said. "I figured I was put paid of you two years ago, and it was fine with me. The orders to bring you in on this came from way upstairs. Getting you in here was not, believe me, my idea."

"Well, maybe you'd better refresh some upstairs memories. I quit, resigned, turned in my secret decoder ring and my Dick Tracy ID card. I'm a Texas cattle rancher. I am *not* a federal agent."

"Were you ever?" Peter said, with a hint of a smile. "You broke every rule written, and you should be long dead in your grave. Lord above, you were a maverick, a rebel born. It's because of you that I'm bald, you know."

Call chuckled. The accompanying smile that appeared, then was gone in the next instant, briefly accentuated the crinkling lines by his eyes.

"So you've said," Call said, "at least a couple of hundred times."

"I've missed you, boy," Peter said quietly. "It's damn good to see you."

"Yeah, I should have kept in touch with you, Pete. It wasn't personal, my not contacting you the past two years. I'd had enough of the agency, that's all, and you are the agency."

"I understand." Peter paused. "Hear tell you've got a fine spread."

"It's coming right along," Call said, nodding. "It's a good life on that land, peaceful, orderly. I owe a lot to Lupe and José, my housekeeper and foreman.

They're married and feel as though that ranch is their home. They agreed to stay on when I bought the place at an estate sale. I'd swear that José knows every damn inch of the ground those acres cover.''

''Well, I'm glad you've found a place where you're comfortable, Call. You're due. No, you're overdue, to settle in. But—''

''Pete,'' Call interrupted, ''whatever it is you want me to do for the agency, the answer is no. I'm not getting sucked back in.''

Peter MacIntosh rested his elbows on the arms of his leather chair and made a steeple of his hands, lightly tapping the tips of his fingers together in a steady rhythm. His bland expression was met by Call Shannon's determined one.

Call Shannon, Peter thought. He'd be—yes, thirty-six years old now. They'd had a strange relationship all these years. He and Call were a war waiting to happen whenever they were together.

Yet they had a deep-seated respect for each other that was simply there, never once spoken aloud in all the years past, but there. And they each knew that if it came right down to the wire, they'd risk their own life to save the other's.

Big, strong, strapping Call, Peter mused. Handsome devil, with rugged, craggy features and thick, black hair, eyes as dark as a raven's wing, body taut, reflexes sharp, mind like a steel trap. Oh, yes, he was a fine man, though a closed, private, solitary man, and Peter—as a father would a son—loved him.

''Taking a nap, Pete?'' Call said. ''I've got a ranch to run that's an hour's hot drive from here. I didn't drag my tired body and my horse dung boots into Houston to listen to you snore. I came to tell you in person to go to hell, and to not contact me again about any of your so-called emergencies.''

"Fair enough. You've told me," Peter said, nodding. "Now that we've gotten all the friendly greetings and social graces out of the way, I'll tell you what this mess is all about."

"No. I'm not listening to a word. Anyway, my security clearance has lapsed. You could get yourself in a heap of trouble sharing classified information with me. You'd better give thought to that fact."

"I'm worried," Peter said dryly. "I'm just shaking in my shorts." He leaned forward and folded his hands loosely on the top of the desk. "Besides, you're forgetting these orders came from way upstairs. When it comes to you, they don't care—'' he glanced at Call's boots "—if your clearance expired. You're the one they want on this. The *only* one."

Call dropped his boot to the floor and got to his feet in a smooth motion. He strode across the plush carpeting, his long legs quickly covering the distance to the windows. Shoving his hands into the back pockets of his soft, faded jeans, he stared unseeingly at the surging traffic below.

Dark images flitted in his mind's eye. Memories that had never totally been forgotten reared their ugly heads to taunt him, causing a painful knot to tighten in his gut.

He knew, without MacIntosh spelling it out, that if the faceless men in their ivory tower, who held other men's lives in their uncaring hands, wanted only him involved in this assignment, that it had something to do with Brian Larson.

He had no intention, Call silently vowed, of allowing Brian's ghost, Brian's betrayal, Brian's shadow, that always hovered cruelly in a corner of Call's mind, to lure him back into the world that he'd escaped from two years before.

Call pulled his hands free of his pockets, then crossed his arms over his chest, as he turned to face Peter. The material of Call's faded blue Western shirt strained against the width of his shoulders and depth of his chest. The sleeves of the shirt were rolled to midforearm, revealing tanned skin, a smattering of dark hair and ropy muscles. His callused hands were large, the fingers long, and blunt on the ends. Black brows knitted in a frown above his obsidian eyes.

Peter swiveled in his chair and met Call's gaze. Silence hung heavily in the air. Call finally took a deep breath and let it out slowly.

"Brian Larson," he said, a steely edge to his voice.

Peter nodded once, his eyes never leaving Call's.

"He's dead, Pete," Call said. "He's two years in the ground."

"Yes."

"He's dead." Pain flickered across Call's face and settled with stark rawness in his eyes. "Oh, yeah, I know that he's dead, because I'm the one who pulled the trigger on the gun that killed him."

Peter sighed. "When are you going to let the misplaced guilt go, boy? You had no choice. Brian Larson was a traitor to his country, as well as to you, his best friend since childhood. It was kill or be killed yourself by him. He's still got a cold fist clutching your soul, Call, and you've got to put an end to it, find the peace you deserve to have."

"Yeah, right," he said, with a snort of disgust. "That's why you sent for me to deal with some garbage that Brian left behind, so I could forget it all that much quicker. Hell.''

"Call, no one can order you to take this assignment. You're a private citizen who owns a cattle ranch. I'll tell the powers that be that you flatly refused to become involved, and that will be that.''

Call narrowed his eyes. "Nice speech, MacIntosh. What's the kicker? Come on, cut to the chase. Let's hear the line you think you're going to reel me in with.''

Peter chuckled and shook his head. "You're not very trusting, boy.''

"Nope.''

"All right, Call. I'll tell you the whole thing, knowing full well that you won't take the assignment. I don't want to dig up painful memories for you of Brian, but maybe you'll be able to offer some advice as to how to handle this.''

Call stared at Peter for a long, silent moment, before returning to slouch in the chair in front of the desk. He resumed his original pose of one booted foot propped on his other knee.

Pete shot the offending boot a dark look, then met Call's eyes.

"You know that Brian Larson," Peter said quietly, "was a traitor to his country, was selling top-secret information to the highest bidder.''

Call did not respond. He once again tugged his Stetson low onto his forehead, and laced his fingers on his chest. He appeared totally relaxed, could even be thought to be dozing if it wasn't for the muscle jumping in his tightly clenched jaw.

"You, Call," Peter continued, "were the first to catch the discrepancies in what Brian was saying and doing. Like most heavy-duty liars, he finally couldn't keep straight what he had said to whom. You followed him that last night on pure gut instinct, with the feeling that he simply wasn't going where he'd said and—"

"I know all this, Pete," Call interrupted. "I've seen this movie, remember? If I didn't like the ending then, I'm sure as hell not going to care for it now."

"I'm sorry. You're right in that you of all people don't need a rehash of what you're very aware of. What's important is the new development. Our people have gotten their hands on one of the men Brian was selling information to. The guy—his name is Solvok—is cooperating from here to Toledo with the hope of getting political asylum in this country. Solvok was to pay Brian a huge sum of money for a list of the names of our agents in Bogan. Those agents would be killed, Solvok would be rewarded with a promotion—everyone would be happy."

Call muttered a word that was a socially unacceptable substitute for describing the less-than-fragrant addition to his boots.

"Anyway," Peter said, "there was a successful coup overthrowing the rulers of Bogan. Solvok and his cronies went underground, and stayed low for the past two years. Solvok has finally surfaced, and he's now telling us that he never received that list of our agents' names from Brian. He paid Brian half of the money up front because they'd done business before without a hitch, but the government was overthrown before Brian delivered. Solvok says Brian told him that if something went wrong, Brian's wife would have a duplicate of the list."

Call straightened in his chair. "Brian didn't have a wife."

"Yes, he did. The agency sure as hell didn't know about it, but he was married in Dallas three months before you...before he died. Brian didn't fill out the necessary papers so that his wife would receive benefits due her. It took some real digging to verify that she actually exists. She does."

"And?"

"And what's her role in this? Does she have that list? Is she waiting for the right time to sell it to the highest bidder? We're moving agents around, shifting new faces into Bogan—you know the routine. But out of Bogan or in, those men and women are still in danger. Is Brian's widow an innocent pawn? Does she have the list, but doesn't realize what it is? Does a duplicate list actually exist, or was Brian blowing smoke? And why keep a new bride a secret, especially from you, his best friend?"

"Okay, okay, give it a rest," Call said, raising one hand. "You've made your point that a great many questions can be asked about this. So do an in-depth intelligence check on this woman, see what you find."

"We already did that, Call. She grew up in poverty in a hole-in-the-wall town near El Paso with a younger brother and a drunken father. The mother cut out when the kids were two and four. Brian's widow's name is Haven. Haven Larson. She's using his name, and I can't say that I blame her for not wanting to be connected to her maiden name of Baxter. There can't be peaceful or pleasant memories there."

"What do you mean?"

"When Haven was sixteen, her father, driving drunk as a skunk, smashed into a vehicle carrying a

couple and three young children. Everyone, including
Haven's father, was killed.''

"Rough."

"Yes. Haven quit school to work and keep food on
the table for her fourteen-year-old brother. How they
slipped past the system and foster homes, I don't
know. Her brother, Ted, was in trouble more than he
was out of it. He had a rap sheet as long as your arm.

"About two and a half years ago, Ted was nailed for
holding up a liquor store. Just before his trial, the
owner of the store dropped all charges, said he'd made
a mistake when he'd picked Ted out of the lineup.
Haven married Brian right after that. Brian was dead
in three months. A month later Ted was killed while
robbing a grocery store. Haven moved here to Houston where she works in a boutique and lives very quietly. That's it—that's all we know.''

"How old is she now?''

"Twenty-five. I have a picture of her in the slim file
we managed to put together. Would you like to see the
photograph?''

"No, MacIntosh," Call said, a weary quality to his
voice, "I don't want to see a photo of Haven Larson.
I don't want to hear any more about Haven Larson, or
her connection to Brian, or any of it. You know, and
I know, that the timing of the liquor store holdup
charges against Ted Baxter being dropped, and Brian's
marriage to Haven warrant a closer look. Maybe it's
a coincidence, but added in with Brian keeping Haven's existence a secret from me and the agency, the
whole enchilada smells funny.''

"I wholeheartedly agree, but gathering the pieces to
put a puzzle like this together is slow work, often with
many false leads and dead ends. Time is of the es-

sence, Call. The lives of the agents whose names are on that list might be in jeopardy. We have got to determine if Haven Larson has that information, and exactly what her role in all of this is."

"Good idea," Call said blandly.

"I suppose we could say that if Haven hasn't done anything with the list in the past two years, she isn't going to. However, that is not a risk we're willing to run."

"Well, I wish you the best of luck with this one, Pete." Call dropped his foot to the floor, indicating that he was about to rise, then hesitated. "Just out of curiosity, why do the big boys think I could get the information they want from this Haven? I don't know her. I didn't even know she existed until a few minutes ago. Any agent could go in and do what I could."

"The rationale is that you were Brian's best friend. If Haven is a foreign agent, she will have been extensively drilled in minute details about Larson in the event that someone like you might come along. After all, she supposedly knew him well enough to have fallen in love with him and married him. But when did she get to know him? He'd been overseas more often than not. It would take you to trip her up, Call."

Call planted his hands on his thighs and leveled himself to his feet. He took off his Stetson, raked one hand through his thick, dark hair, then settled the hat firmly back on his head.

"Nice chatting with you, Pete," he said. "You're as dapper as always, spit shined and pretty. See ya." He started across the room.

"Call," Peter said quietly. "There's something else that I haven't told you."

Call stopped, turned and shook his head, an expression of disgust on his face.

"Ah, the ace in the hole," he said, his voice ringing with sarcasm. "The zinger that's going to make me put out my hand and ask for the file on Haven Larson because I've decided—due to this last news flash—to take the assignment. Not a chance. I'm outta here, Pete. I'm going home to the Triple S where I belong, where I want to be. There's nothing you could say that could sucker punch me into taking this on. Nothing."

Peter got slowly to his feet and walked to the gleaming windows. He stared out, not at the city as Call had done, but up to the heavens, and the brilliant blue sky that was dotted with fluffy, white clouds.

"Haven Larson—" he started, then turned to look at Call "—has a daughter. Brian's baby. We now know that Brian told Solvok that Haven had a duplicate list. How many other people have gotten wind of that? Whether Haven is guilty or innocent, Call, that child's life could very well be at risk."

Memories slammed against Call's brain with excruciating pain, accompanied by anger so intense that it created a momentary red haze to blur his vision. His hands curled into tight fists at his sides and a pulse beat wildly at his temple.

"Damn you, MacIntosh," he said, his voice raspy. "Damn you straight to hell." He drew a shuddering breath. "Give me . . . give me Haven Larson's file."

A few minutes later, the door to Peter's office was slammed shut as Call left without a further word, the file bending from the force of the ironlike grip of his hand.

A heavy silence fell over the lush expanse.

"I'm sorry, Call," Peter said, to the empty room. "God help me, boy, I'm so damn sorry."

Two

Call pushed open the screen door and stepped out onto the good-size back porch, leaving the brightly lit, large kitchen of the ranch house. He walked slowly across the wooden structure, then stopped, leaning one shoulder against the support post next to the steps.

The porch boasted a cedar swing built to hold two people, and suspended by chains from the cross-beams. He had crafted the swing by hand, sanding the rich wood until it was satin smooth.

Many evenings he would settle onto the swing, moving it lazily back and forth with one booted foot as he unwound from his long, busy day. But tonight he was edgy, restless, and knew that if he sat down, he'd be on his feet again within moments.

He took a deep breath to inhale and savor the scents of the warm night: the heady aroma of cattle he could hear lowing in the distance, freshly cut hay, earth and water, man and beast.

Stars in the summer sky were like a multitude of sparkling diamonds, and fireflies danced through the air as though inviting the stars to drop from the heavens and play a game of tag.

Call's next breath was a sigh; a weary-sounding sigh, that seemed to come from the very depths of his soul. The peace he usually found as he stood there after dinner eluded him, taunted him by hovering just beyond his reach.

Haven Larson, he thought. He had yet to open the file he'd thrown onto the desk in his office that afternoon, had yet to put a face with the name, bring the past firmly into the present.

Damn her for existing, for having married and given birth to Brian's child. Damn her for raking up the ashes of the hell within him whose fire of pain was never totally extinguished.

Was she as guilty as Brian had been? Or was she an innocent pawn? He had to know, he *would* know. And there, always there, in the front of his mind, was the fact that a baby was caught in the center of what might be an evil web of danger and deception. Damn.

"Call," a woman said, bringing him from his troubled thoughts. "The kitchen is clean, spic-span."

He turned to see a short, plump Mexican woman in her early fifties silhouetted in the doorway.

"Thank you, Lupe," he said. "I won't need anything else tonight. You go on to your cottage. I imagine that José is hungry for his dinner."

"Oh, that José," she said, smiling. "He always hungry as a buffalo."

"Bear," Call said. "Hungry as a bear."

"Bear," she said, nodding. *"Sí."* She paused. "Call, you have sad heart this night? You have no smile, only frown."

"No, no, I'm fine. I just have things to think about, that's all. Don't worry about me."

"Who will worry if Lupe doesn't? You need wife, babies, smiling and laughing, in this big house. You alone too much, Call Shannon."

"So you've said many times." He chuckled. "Stop fussing, and go feed your husband."

"I go, I go, but you smile."

"Yes, I'll smile. Good night."

"Good night."

Moments later the kitchen light went out, and the darkness on the porch deepened along with the frown on Call's face.

A wife, babies, laughing in that big house, his mind echoed. Many, *many,* years ago he'd pictured a wife and children as part of his life as a matter of course, the natural order of things. But he'd chosen a different path, a dark road, where no room existed to surround himself with a family.

And now? It was too late. There were too many chilling shadows hovering around his soul, layered too deeply for the warmth of a woman's love and the laughter of happy children to break through. He was alone, and would remain alone, there on the Triple S.

He'd bought the ranch two years ago when he'd walked away from the world of death, lies, hate and guilt. He worked hard on his land, and reaped the rewards of his labor. This was where he belonged now, where he'd found as much inner peace as he'd ever be able to obtain. This was his home, his safe haven, his . . .

Haven.

Ah, hell, he thought, even her name tripped him up, dragged him to a place he had no wish to travel to. Haven Larson. He couldn't put it off any longer. He had to read the file.

With heavy steps and a tight set to his jaw, Call entered the house and made his way to his office where the wrinkled file lay waiting.

Haven Larson handed the pale pink bag to the elegantly dressed woman in her forties.

"There you are, Mrs. Emerson," Haven said. "I know you'll be pleased with the camisoles and tap pants. That peach shade you chose is lovely."

"I want Billy to be more than pleased," Mrs. Emerson said, laughing. "I've been too complacent lately. It's time to put some zing back into my marriage, let my Billy know I'm not taking him for granted. These satin and lace undies ought to do the trick. Thanks for your help, Haven. I'll report back to you on my success. Before I'm finished, Billy Emerson is going to remember there's more to life than oil wells. Ta-ta."

"Goodbye," Haven said.

Her smile faded as the tinkling bell above the closing door stilled, and silence fell over the boutique.

Billy Emerson, she mused, was a lucky man. He was deeply loved by a beautiful woman who had the aura of grace and class that seemed a natural part of the wealthy. Mrs. Emerson would most definitely make her Billy forget about his oil wells for a while.

Oil wells, Haven thought, with a shake of her head, and yachts, homes as large as hotels, private planes, chauffeurs for limousines... The list went on. Those

were the type of women who came into the store, the
Pot of Gold. Those were the ones who stood on the
other side of the counter from Haven and bought
the outrageously priced lingerie and accessories.

Her own world was far different from theirs. She
could not, in fact, really imagine what it might be like
to exist in the monied arena where the patrons of the
shop moved as naturally as breathing.

Did she envy them? Oh, at times, she supposed,
when she struggled to stretch her paycheck one to the
next. And at times, she supposed, when she witnessed
a love, a marriage, as strong and real as the Emer-
sons'.

But in the broad picture? No, she wouldn't trade
places with any of the rich and famous who shopped
at the Pot of Gold. No, because in her world was
Paige, her precious baby, her adorable eighteen-
month-old daughter. Money and social status meant
nothing compared to Paige.

A gentle smile formed on Haven's lips as she saw
Paige so clearly in her mind's eye, it was as though she
could reach out and gather the baby close, inhale her
aroma of powder, lotion and innocence. Paige's nonsensical chatter echoed in Haven's heart, along with
the joyful sound of her child's laughter.

Haven's smile faded as her mind skittered into the
shadows of the past, of the dark, fearful time before
the emergence of Paige into her life.

No, she wouldn't dwell on all that, she told herself.
It served no purpose, as the memories were painful,
lonely and stark. Her life in the sunshine had begun on
the day Paige was born. They were a team. The two of
them would tackle life's problems together.

And as Paige's mother, Haven vowed, she would protect, love and cherish her precious human gift for all time. Nothing, nor no one, would ever, *ever*, harm her Paige. The baby would grow up knowing that she was loved, and secure in the knowledge that Haven's love was strong enough to let her daughter go when it was time.

Paige might not have all the materialistic things her friends did over the years, but the love would be there, always.

Haven's reverie was halted by the entrance of two young women who were carrying shopping bags from several exclusive boutiques.

"Good afternoon," Haven said, a smile matching her pleasant tone of voice. "May I help you?"

"We'll browse first, then buy," one of the women said. "Definitely buy. Our husbands will think twice about spending yet another day on the golf course when they get the bills from this shopping spree."

"Amen to that," the other woman said, laughing. "We'll have gotten across the fact that we're feeling neglected, and have new clothes thrown in for good measure."

But neither one of them, Haven thought, would have Paige.

Call stood in a small park across the street from the Pot of Gold. He'd been there for over an hour, one shoulder propped casually against the trunk of a tree, a nondescript expression on his face.

If anyone bothered to wonder why he was there, they'd no doubt come to the conclusion that his wife, lover, whomever, was shopping in one of the multitude of expensive stores in that area, and he'd chosen to wait in the park.

That he was not dressed to the nines would not draw suspicious glances, as true Texans knew that the condition of a cowboy's clothes at a given moment was not necessarily a declaration of his monetary status.

That Call's jeans were faded to the point of white in places, his boots scuffed, that his Western shirt might one day have been a vibrant shade of blue, but was now a rather dingy gray, gave no real clue to his tax bracket.

To some men, their boots were of prime importance. They might come into town in mud-splattered jeans, but would have first changed into their finest, spit-shined boots.

Another cowboy might center his attention on his belt buckle, especially if it announced that he was a rodeo winner.

Call Shannon took pride in his Stetson. He'd owned it for many years, knowing it represented his dream, his goal, the life he would lead when he retired from government service.

The hat had often hung for months in his furnished room in Washington, D.C., while he'd been away on assignment. He'd return, weary in mind and body, and place the Stetson on his head, telling himself that he was just that much closer to his dream.

Call shifted his weight slightly against the tree, and tugged the Stetson farther down on his forehead. The hat was coal black and as soft to the touch as a pretty woman's skin. The band was made of small conchas, hand-tooled from the finest silver. That Stetson held its shape and texture despite nature's abuse of wind, dust, rain and snow.

Damn fine Stetson, Call thought, running a fingertip along the front brim. He was keeping it firmly on his head today to reassure himself that he really was a Texas rancher, and *not* a government agent. This assignment would be short, very temporary, and he'd be sleeping every night in his own bed where he belonged.

It wouldn't take him long to discover if Haven Larson had really known Brian well enough to fall in love with him and agree to marry him.

If she tripped herself up on details, he'd know that the marriage had been a sham, a means to an end. That Haven had cut a deal with Brian would be obvious; the charges against her brother had been dropped.

But how much more was Haven involved in? Just what part did she play in regard to that list?

Well, one piece of the puzzle at a time. First up was to put the grieving widow through her paces on details about her darling husband. It wouldn't take long at all to properly judge Mrs. Larson's true knowledge of her husband, because Call had known Brian, loved Brian, like a brother.

He had also killed Brian Larson by pulling the trigger of a gun.

Call muttered an earthy expletive and eased himself away from the tree.

He did *not* want to be here. He'd like to dump the whole mess back into MacIntosh's lap. He'd also like to wring Peter's neck for pushing the one emotional button that Call had no defense against: the baby. Haven Larson had an innocent little baby.

On the chance, *slim chance,* that Haven was a pawn in one of Brian's double-crossing games, then it would be up to Call to protect her and the child. If Haven was a foreign agent, then he'd see to it that the baby was placed in a proper home.

Nothing—*nothing* was going to happen to that innocent baby.

He'd watched the boutique long enough, he decided. There was no particular pattern to the customer traffic. No men had gone in, but one was about to, and from the looks of the frilly, fancy underthings in the window, he was going to appear very out of place in the Pot of Gold.

Haven smiled as she looked out of the front window of the boutique.

Well, well, she thought, the cowboy wasn't permanently attached to the tree after all.

She'd noticed him when he'd first arrived in the park, her attention caught by his build and easy, rolling gait. She was too far away to see his features clearly, but she'd decided, for the lack of anything better to do at that moment, that he was certainly nicely put together. His shoulders were wide, hips narrow, he was tall and, oh my, that sexy walk.

She'd made a silly game of checking on him during the past hour when she wasn't busy with customers. Before very long, she'd marveled at his ability to remain so perfectly still.

At times she'd gotten the impression that he was looking directly at her through the store window. But that, she'd reasoned, was simply her conscience pricking her, as she'd never before indulged in such blatant man watching.

And now the cowboy had straightened, had finally unglued himself from the trunk of the tree.

Haven's eyes widened, and she drew a sharp breath.

He was crossing the street and heading right for the Pot of Gold. No, that was nonsense. He'd turn once he got to the sidewalk. A man came into the shop occasionally, but was usually accompanied by a woman. The few men who'd entered alone had been wearing thousand-dollar suits and Rolex watches.

Cowboys, and this was an authentic, working cowboy, did not patronize the Pot of Gold. She'd lived in Texas all of her life, and could tell the difference between real and store-bought cowboys at a glance.

But, no, he wasn't turning. He was staying on course right to the front of the store, was now reaching for the doorknob, and . . .

Call stepped into the Pot of Gold, closed the door behind him and immediately looked down at his boots as they sank into the thick, plush carpeting. Soft music could just barely be heard floating through the air, and the faint, sweet aroma of flowers reached him.

His eyes swept quickly over the interior, seeing the rainbow of colors used to create the vast array of fancy lingerie.

He idly wondered what some of the skimpy pieces of satin and lace cost, then decided in the next instant that he didn't want to know.

And then his gaze collided with Haven Larson's. He felt an unexpected jolt, and a very unwelcomed tightening coil of heat deep and low in his body.

Her picture in MacIntosh's file, Call realized, had not begun—*not even close*—to do her justice. The snapshot had been rather blurry, and showed an attractive, but not knock-'em-dead woman, with a wild tumble of blond curls that fell to her shoulders. In the picture, she'd been wearing cutoff jeans and an oversize T-shirt. She'd been smiling, appeared young and carefree, and if she had a nice figure, the baggy T-shirt hid it well.

He had not, Call admitted to himself, been prepared for the Haven Larson who stood behind that counter. This Haven was beautiful.

Her hair was now worn short, the soft blond curls framing her face and complementing her delicate features. She had the biggest eyes he'd ever seen, and they were as blue as a Texas summer sky.

The pale pink dress she wore was simple, yet managed to accentuate her nicely proportioned figure. She was holding his gaze steadily with hers, a slight lift to her chin that was an unspoken message of her determination not to be the first to break the contact.

"May I help you?" Haven said, bringing Call abruptly from his mental ramblings.

He started slowly across the carpeted expanse.

Oh, good night, Haven thought, feeling a funny flutter dance along her spine, he was incredible. His features were rough-hewn, craggy, as though chiseled from stone, not fully smoothed by the artist's hand, then bronzed. His high cheekbones, square jaw and chin, the blade cut of his nose, plus sensuous lips, all added magnificently to his blatant masculinity.

And, oh, dear heaven, that walk, that loose-hipped, easy rolling, cowboy walk.

Call stopped at the counter, then pushed up his Stetson a tad with one thumb.

"Ma'am," he said, touching the brim of the hat for an instant with his index finger.

Haven acknowledged the greeting with a slight dip of her head, knowing the gesture had been the height of politeness to true men of the West. That he had not removed his hat upon entering the shop did not indicate lack of respect, nor less than socially acceptable manners. A cowboy simply didn't take his hat from his head without definite just cause.

"Was there something in particular that I could show you," Haven said, "or would you prefer to browse?"

Call glanced around once again, frowned, then redirected his attention to Haven.

"I didn't come in here to shop," he said. "The fact is, word just reached me that you existed, and I decided to drop by and say hello."

"That I existed?" Haven repeated, obviously confused. "I don't understand."

"You're Brian Larson's wife...widow," Call said quietly.

Haven's eyes widened in shock, and she gripped the edge of the counter so tightly, her knuckles turned white. A buzzing noise roared in her ears, strange black spots danced before her eyes and she swayed unsteadily on her feet.

"Whoa," Call said. His hands shot out to grasp her shoulders, the counter separating them causing him to swear under his breath. If Haven Larson fainted dead out on him, he'd have no choice but to lean as far over the counter as possible, then finally let her slip onto the floor. "Stay with me here. Steady now. Ma'am? Mrs. Larson? Haven? Haven?"

She blinked, drew a shuddering breath, then met his troubled gaze.

"Yes," she whispered. "Yes, I'm all right. You just...startled me. I haven't heard his name in so long and... Who are you?"

Call slowly released his hold on her, keeping his hands in the air next to her shoulders for an extra moment to assure himself that she was once again in control. He straightened, then shoved his hands into the back pockets of his jeans.

"I'm Call Shannon," he said. He watched her face, her eyes, for any sign, the smallest flicker of recognition at the announcement of his name. He saw none. "Brian and I grew up together in Austin, were best friends until he..." Until he turned into a traitor to his country. Until Call had shot him dead. "He died."

"I see," Haven said. She could still feel the strength, the warmth, of Call Shannon's hands where they'd gripped her shoulders with a strong, yet gentle touch. They were large hands, work-roughened hands and, dear Lord, the incredible heat of them. "Well, I'm afraid he never mentioned you to me, Mr. Shannon."

"Call. Brian never bored you to sleep with all the stories of our wild escapades as boys? That's surprising. He enjoyed telling those tales over and over."

Haven pulled her gaze from Call's and began to fiddle with the business cards that were in a clear plastic holder next to the cash register.

"No, he didn't share those stories with me. Well, Mr. Shannon..."

"Call."

She looked up at him again.

"Call. Thank you for stopping by. It was nice to meet a friend of Brian's. I hope you're not offended to think that he never mentioned you, but he was working on a complicated... project during the short time we had together, and was very preoccupied. So it was nothing personal. I'm sure he valued your long-standing friendship a great deal. Now, I really must get back to work. Thank you again for your thoughtful visit. I—"

"You'd better grab some air there before you get the vapors, or whatever. That was a long spiel on one breath. You were suddenly chattering like a magpie. Do I make you nervous?"

Haven glared at him. "Don't be silly." Go away, Call Shannon. Oh, she just wished he'd go away and leave her alone. She didn't want to talk about Brian, be reminded that Brian Larson ever existed. "Goodbye."

"Well, now, Haven, ma'am," Call said, "*goodbye* is a real final-sounding word. I believe I'll settle for something closer to 'See you later,' instead."

"No, I think not, Mr. Shannon."

"Call. And, ma'am? *I* think yes, so that makes it a fact that you can take all the way to the bank."

"Now wait just a minute here," Haven said, anger flashing in her blue eyes. "I have a voice in who I see, speak to, choose to—"

"Y'all have a real nice day, darlin'," Call interrupted, one index finger touching the brim of his hat.

He turned and strode across the store, then went out the door without a backward glance.

Haven wrapped her hands around her elbows in a protective gesture as a chill, a shiver of fear, swept through her.

Three

Call drained the last of the strong, bitter coffee from the heavy, beige mug. Then he set the mug on the wooden tabletop with a thud. The small café was nearly empty, affording him the near silence he'd sought to sift through the data in his mind.

He'd driven away from the affluent neighborhood where the Pot of Gold was located, to a section of the city that exhibited evidence of wear, age and the broken dreams of those who lived in the narrow, dingy tenements.

The café he'd entered was like the multitude he'd been in around the globe. The aroma of grease hung heavily in the air, the faded, red vinyl seats in the booths were cracked and torn, some crisscrossed with stiff, black electrician's tape.

The tables had messages carved into the surfaces,

declaring undying love between unknown people whose initials were there for all time.

To Call, the café was real, earthy and existed in a world he understood and could relate to. It was here that he'd chosen to evaluate his encounter with Haven Larson.

Haven, his brain thundered, for the umpteenth time. Damn, each attempt to analytically dissect the interchange at the Pot of Gold was pulled off course as images of Haven—the woman—flitted in his mental vision. The details of what had been said, what he had observed, were blurred by Haven herself.

This wasn't like him, not one damn bit. He had perfected his objectivity years before, was totally capable of detaching facts from any emotional pull that might be caused by the person those facts were pertaining to.

But not this time. Haven insisted on getting in the way, cluttering the path between making the discovery and drawing a conclusion.

So far, the conclusions he *had* come to were slim, practically nothing. He was very certain that his name had not been familiar to Haven, and her extreme reaction to his reference to Brian had been an honest display of shock.

Beyond that, all he really knew was that Haven was lovely, desirable, had a streak of feisty temper, a quiet aura of vulnerability and she was driving him out of his ever-lovin' mind.

When he'd leaned across the counter to grasp her shoulders, he'd been acutely aware of how delicate she was. A man with any strength at all would have to temper that power with gentleness when he touched her, drew her into his embrace, made love....

"Shut up, Shannon," he muttered, feeling a tightening low in his body. "Just shut the hell up."

With a disgusted shake of his head, he drummed the fingers of one hand restlessly on top of the scarred table.

Get it together, he directed himself. He was two years rusty at putting into practice his fine-tuned training and experience. That was perfectly understandable. It was no big deal, now that he realized what was happening. His expertise and objectivity would kick in any second now. No problem.

Haven, he mused on. She had the biggest blue eyes he'd ever seen. They'd pinned him in place, caused heat to course through him, had made him feel as though he was drowning in those summer-sky pools.

And her lips? Oh, hell, those lips were made for kissing. They were perfectly shaped, appeared soft, feminine, had been beckoning him to capture them with his own.

"More coffee, sweetheart?"

Call's head snapped around to look at the waitress, realizing that she was not the one who had originally taken his order. This woman, he decided, was forty-plus and fighting it. Her hair was dyed too red, her make-up was too heavy, her uniform too tight, straining over bulges she was trying to ignore. There was a deep weariness evident in her eyes, but her wide smile was genuine, and Call liked her on sight.

"No, thanks, darlin'," he said, smiling at her. "That stuff makes battery acid sound appealing."

"This here's a fresh pot, honey," she said, filling his mug. "Sweet Ginger—that's me, Ginger—made this one. When I make coffee, cowboy, you've got yourself a fine mug of brew."

"There you go," he said, nodding. "Appreciate it."

"You bet, sugar." She started away, then stopped, looking back at Call over one shoulder. "Is she really worth it?"

"What?"

"Honey, if I ever saw a man with heart trouble eatin' at him, it's you. Can't imagine a woman fool enough to give fits to a fella the likes of you but . . . Well, I sure do hope she's worth it." She sashayed away, adding an extra wiggle to her ample hips.

Heart trouble? Call's mind echoed. Over Haven Larson? No. Not a chance. Sweet Ginger had sized up his preoccupation totally wrong. He was a highly trained, albeit a tad rusty, ex-government agent, who was concentrating on evaluating a series of facts. And that, thank you very much, was that.

Call took a sip of the hot coffee, a smile tugging onto his lips as he realized immediately that it tasted worse than the first batch. He set the drink aside, and stared out the dirty window.

He had to plan his next move. He'd made it clear as he'd left Haven that he'd be seeing her again. That pushy announcement had ignited her temper, caused laser beams to flash in those incredible blue eyes.

Call frowned.

Wait a minute. There was something nagging at him, hovering in the back of his mind. It . . . yes, there it was. There'd been more than anger in Haven's eyes. There'd been fear, as well.

Damn, he thought, running one hand across his chin, he'd frightened her with his threat to reappear.

Well, fine, that was fine, he reasoned. She *should* be scared if she had something to hide, if she was every bit as guilty as Brian had been.

But if she wasn't guilty? What then? Then he was a jerk for frightening her, for causing the fear he'd seen in those gorgeous blue eyes.

If she was innocent, then she was simply what she appeared to be: a single mother, who was working hard to support her child. She didn't deserve to be hassled by a stranger who suddenly appeared out of nowhere, bringing with him ghosts of the past. Lord, he was lower than dirt.

No, damn it, he was just doing his job, that's all. He hadn't asked for this assignment, and heaven knew he sure didn't want it, but it was his now to see through to its proper end.

But he could not remember ever being this torn about what he was doing. Haven Larson had nudged awake something, *something* within him that he hadn't even known was there and asleep. He was not a happy man about that little news flash. Not even close.

With a muttered expletive, he slid out of the booth and dropped several bills onto the table. He started toward the door.

"Y'all come visit your Ginger again when you want a good cup of coffee, cowboy," the waitress said.

"See ya, Ginger," Call said, touching the brim of his Stetson.

"There was a time, cowboy," she said softly as he was leaving, "when you would have come back, when I was young and pretty."

When Call glanced back he saw she'd stopped clearing the table, her thoughts centered on days long past, but not forgotten.

Just after six o'clock, Haven turned the key in the dead bolt of the back door of the boutique. She started across the parking lot, then came to a complete halt after going no more than ten steps.

Her eyes widened in shock, and her heart began to beat with a rapid tattoo.

Call Shannon was leaning casually against her car.

Haven blinked, desperately hoping that she'd imagined that he was there, that he was simply invading her mental vision the way he'd done the entire afternoon.

But this time, she realized instantly, the image of Call was not a product of her wayward and maddening imagination. He was really there, looking so darn big and intimidating, and so darn ruggedly handsome, *and so darn male*.

His backside was resting against her blue compact car, and his arms were folded loosely over his broad chest. One booted foot crossed the other. His Stetson was low on his forehead, shadowing his face and making it impossible to read any expression that might be there.

He was masculinity personified, Haven thought, unable to ignore the funny flutter that danced along her spine. But more than that, he was a threat to her peace of mind, her tranquil existence. Call Shannon had known Brian, known him very well for many years. Call was attempting to bring the past into her present, and she was not going to allow him to do that.

She squared her shoulders, lifted her chin and marched forward.

There was about to be hell to pay, Call thought. Lord, Haven Larson was sensational. She was advancing like the troops at Gettysburg, ready to do battle. She was dynamite waiting to explode, all wrapped up in a delectable, feminine package. And she was causing heat to coil tight and low in his aching body.

Haven stopped a foot away from Call.

"Mr. Shannon," she said stiffly, "kindly get your tush off my car. Now."

Call touched the brim of his Stetson. "Evenin', ma'am," he drawled, not moving. "Sure is a nice summer night, isn't it?"

"It was," she said, lifting her chin another notch, "until I saw you out here. Move. I'm not going to say it again."

"That's good," he said. "Much more, and you'd begin to sound real naggy."

Haven rolled her eyes heavenward, then looked at him again.

"You're rude," she said, "and arrogant, and cocky."

"That about covers it," he said, nodding. "Now that we've got that out of the way, how would you like to go have a bite to eat?"

"Are you out of your tiny mind?" she said, nearly shrieking. "Just who in the blue blazes do you think you are, mister?"

Call shoved up his Stetson, and met her angry glare. There was no hint of a smile on his face, and his voice was very low when he spoke again.

"I was Brian Larson's best friend for many, many years. I don't understand why he didn't tell me about you, but word filtered down, and now I know that you exist. You and I have Brian in common, Haven. I want to talk to you about him for a bit, that's all."

Oh, drat, she thought, Call Shannon didn't play fair. She'd seen, just for a second, a flicker of stark, raw pain in his dark eyes as he'd spoken quietly of Brian. She was a link to Call's childhood friend, a connection to someone he had loved and lost.

Call would never believe her if she said she actually knew very little about Brian Larson. If she refused to talk to Call about Brian, she'd appear to be cold, unfeeling, chalking up Call's loss as unimportant.

For some unexplainable reason, she didn't want Call to think poorly of her. Why it should even matter, she had no idea.

But by the same token, her lack of basic knowledge about Brian would be glaringly evident in a discussion about the man. She had no intention of revealing why she had married Brian, would not subject herself to the painful memories and Call's censure.

Could she fake it? she wondered. Chitchat with Call about Brian by continually urging Call to speak? Well, it was the only option open to her, as she simply couldn't send him on his way without answering his need to discuss his best friend. After seeing that pain in his eyes, she just couldn't do that.

"All right, Call." A sigh of defeat escaped from her lips. "Why don't you follow me home, and we'll talk...briefly."

"Appreciate it," he said. He touched the brim of his hat with one finger as he pushed himself away from her car. "Tell you what. You give me your address—" which he already knew from studying her file "—and I'll pick up some burgers. I'm intruding on your dinner hour, and the least I can do is furnish the meal."

"Oh, well, I don't—" she started, then stopped. Fast food? Burgers, fries and thick, eat-'em-with-a-spoon milk shakes? Heavenly, and not in her budget. It all sounded absolutely delicious. "Okay. Burger, fries, chocolate shake?"

"There you go," he said, smiling. "How about a double order of fries?"

"Sold," she said, matching his smile.

Their eyes met, and their smiles slowly faded. Neither moved, nor hardly breathed. They simply stood there, not aware if seconds, minutes or hours passed.

A sensual current as potent as a downed electric wire crackled through the air, weaving around and through them. Hearts raced, and heat thrummed low in a body soft and feminine, and one ruggedly taut and masculine.

Of its own volition it seemed, Call's right hand lifted; then he drew his thumb lightly over Haven's cheek. It was a simple gesture, a callused thumb stroking velvet-soft skin, yet it caused Haven to tremble and Call to ache with heightened desire. The heat within them grew hotter, bursting into a raging flame.

"Haven," Call said.

The gritty, passion-laden sound of his own voice brought Call from the hazy mist that surrounded them. He jerked his hand away and frowned.

"What's your address?" he said gruffly.

"What's my what?" she said, hearing the thread of breathlessness in her voice. She blinked, then took a step backward. "Oh. My address...yes...I...yes." She rattled off the information. "Goodbye. I mean, I'll see you there in a bit and—goodbye."

She hurried around him, and inserted her key in the car door, unable to ignore the fact that her hand was shaking.

Call shifted enough to look at her for a long moment, then without speaking he spun around and strode to his truck with heavy steps.

He yanked opened the door, slid behind the wheel and pulled the door closed with more force than was necessary. After turning the key in the ignition, he allowed the engine to idle as he waited for Haven to drive out of the parking lot.

As she disappeared from view, Call smacked the steering wheel with the palm of one hand, and cut loose with a string of earthy expletives.

He put the truck into gear and reversed, tires squealing. In the next instant, he slammed on the brakes in self-disgust, bringing the vehicle to a screeching, jarring halt. He automatically glanced behind him to be assured that the battered Winchester rifle was still secure in the gun rack mounted on the inside of the rear window.

Cool it, Shannon, he ordered himself. Driving like a lunatic wasn't the answer to... Hell, the answer to what? Just what had happened in that eerie scene with Haven?

He had never, *ever*, experienced anything like that before. He was a man of control, totally in command of his mind and body. Yet he'd fallen under Haven Larson's spell, been mesmerized by the allure of those big, blue eyes and by the essence of the woman herself.

Damn it, how had that happened? What did it mean?

He didn't know, and he was so angry, thrown so off kilter by the whole episode, that he didn't particularly care *what* it meant.

What he *did* know was the bottom line: it was never going to happen again.

Four

In Haven's mind, the place where she and Paige lived was a cottage—a cute, cozy, little cottage. It was not, she'd decided early on, large enough by any stretch of the imagination to be called a house. Nor was it, to her, an actual apartment. It was, quite simply, a cottage, even though the manager advertised the rental units as freestanding bungalows.

The complex was in the shape of a horseshoe, with a total of six cottages. The open end gave access to the parking lot and a grassy area in the center of the group. The lush, green carpet of grass held two picnic tables, a brick barbecue and a swing set.

Haven parked the car, turned off the ignition, but made no move to open the door. She drew a steadying breath that was threaded with weariness.

Call Shannon, her mind echoed. That was it—just his name, beating against her tired brain. During the drive home, she'd attempted to rehash, dissect and analyze exactly what had happened between her and Call in the parking lot at the boutique. But she'd been unable to get past the repeated drumming of his name. Call Shannon.

Dear Lord, she thought frantically, he was so dangerous. He represented the past, which included Brian and memories she had no wish to relive.

But it went beyond Call's threat to her peaceful existence. In the present, the now, he was jarring her, pushing her sensual buttons, making her acutely aware of her own femininity, her womanliness.

Desire had thrummed deep and hot within her. It was not familiar, nor had she experienced it before, but she'd somehow known that those turbulent sensations were desire.

She wanted Call Shannon.

"No," she said aloud, feeling the warm flush on her cheeks once again.

Shaking her head, she left the car, locking the door behind her. She hurried along the sidewalk fronting the cottages and rimming the grassy courtyard to the bungalow on the farthest side of the back section.

She'd been attempting, she admitted, to outrun her own frightening thoughts, and had failed. She unlocked the door to the cottage and entered.

An instant smile lit up her face, and Call Shannon and the confusion and fear his emergence into her life had caused were momentarily forgotten.

Her focus was centered on the baby toddling toward her with arms held up, and a smile on her precious face. Haven was home, Paige was there and right then, nothing else mattered.

Haven dropped her purse onto the sofa and scooped up her daughter, hugging her tightly, inhaling and savoring her aroma of powder, lotion and soap.

"Mama," Paige said, attempting to wiggle free of the restraining hold. "Mama, Mama."

"Hello, hello, my sweet," Haven said. She set Paige back onto her feet.

"Mama," Paige said. "Chee."

"Oh, you had some cheese?" Haven said.

"Chee," the baby repeated. "Chee, chee."

Haven laughed, then looked up at the woman standing across the room. She was in her late fifties, but her snowy-white hair and wrinkled face caused her to appear older. She was short and plump, and had fit, from the moment Haven had met her, the image of the perfect, quintessential grandmother.

"Hello, Marian," Haven said. "Was Paige a good girl for you today?"

"Oh, she was a darling," Marian said, smiling. "She ate like a little piggy, took a nice long nap and was a happy baby."

"Good."

"Well, I'm off home. Living right next door certainly beats fighting the rush-hour traffic, doesn't it?" Marian laughed. "There I go again. I say that at least three times a week, bless my silly old mind." She picked up a cloth tote bag that was embroidered with brightly colored yarn flowers. "I have my knitting, my romance novel and I'm all set. Do you have plans for the weekend, Haven?"

"Plans? Oh, well, no, not really."

Marian clicked her tongue. "You need to get out, socialize, meet a scrumptious man."

"Here we go again," Haven said, laughing. "You say *that* at least three times a week, too."

"Well, it's true," Marian said, crossing the room. She bent down and kissed the top of Paige's head. "'Bye for now, sweetheart. 'Bye-bye."

"'Bye, bye," Paige repeated, flapping both hands in the air.

Marian waved at the baby, then continued on her way, only to stop again as a knock sounded at the door.

Call, Haven thought, feeling the instant wild beating of her heart. How had he gotten there so quickly? Or had she lost track of time as she'd sat outside in her car when she'd first arrived home? It didn't matter how or why, the fact remained that Call Shannon was standing on the opposite side of that door.

"Haven?" Marian said. "Are you asleep, dear? There's someone knocking on your door."

"What? Well, yes, there certainly is, isn't there?" Haven, shut up. She was blathering like an idiot. "I wonder who—" She threw up her hands. "Forget it."

She moved around Marian and opened the door to find Call holding two large white bags in his arms.

"Hello, Call. Come in," she said, stepping back. "That smells marvelous," she added, as he passed her.

"It's good and hot," he said, as Haven closed the door behind him.

"Marian," Haven said, "this is Call Shannon. Call, meet Marian Smith, my neighbor, friend and Paige's baby-sitter. That short person there is my daughter, Paige."

"Da-da," the baby said, clapping her hands. "Da-da, Da-da." She toddled over to Call and wrapped her arms around one of his knees. "Da-da."

Call smiled down at the baby. "Hi there, kiddo."

"It's a pleasure to meet you, Mr. Shannon," Marian said, beaming.

"Call," he said. "The pleasure is mine, ma'am."

"Da-da," Paige yelled, at the top of her lungs.

Haven cringed and reached for the baby, settling Paige onto her hip. "She's at the stage where she calls every man she sees Da-da. Just ignore it."

Call's smile faded as he looked at the pair.

Paige Larson, he mused, was a tiny version of Haven. With a cap of silky, blond curls, big blue eyes and delicate features, he could see no trace of Brian in the baby. Paige was Haven's. So be it.

"That little girl," he said quietly, "would be impossible to ignore. I didn't know about her but you have a very beautiful daughter, Haven."

"Thank you," she whispered.

"Well, off I go," Marian said, still smiling to beat the band. "Enjoy, just thoroughly enjoy your evening." She left the cottage.

"Where should I put these sacks?" Call said.

"Oh, right over here on the table," Haven said.

She passed in front of him, but didn't even glance at him. He followed her to the dining alcove at the end of the living room and adjacent to the kitchen. He put the sacks on the table and began to unpack them, as Haven slid Paige into her high chair and tied a bib around the baby's neck.

Haven disappeared into the kitchen and reappeared with a damp washcloth and a towel. She wiped and dried Paige's hands, then returned the supplies to the kitchen. Bustling back into the dining area, she sat at the table.

"All set," she said. "This is a real treat. I adore fast food, but my budget says I have to worship it from afar."

Call removed his Stetson and placed it on the empty chair at the end of the table. He sat down across from Haven.

She was nervous, he thought, narrowing his eyes slightly. She was definitely avoiding looking directly at him, was talking too fast and was fluttering around like a jittery butterfly.

Why? Did she feel cornered, trapped, because after two years, a stranger had appeared wanting to talk about Brian? If she was guilty as sin, she might be worried that she'd long since forgotten some of the minuscule details that she'd been programmed with, regarding Brian.

Guilty, his mind echoed. Haven Larson a foreign agent, a traitor to her country, a woman who was not even remotely close to how she was presenting herself? Damn, that was difficult to fathom as he sat there looking at her, watching her interact with her daughter.

But years of experience had taught him that evil came in packages of every size, shape and age. He'd do well to remember that. He'd taken himself in hand as he'd sat in his truck in the parking lot of the boutique. Haven Larson was *not* a woman, she was an assignment.

Haven suddenly laughed as Paige began to beat a rhythm on her high-chair tray, demanding her dinner. An instant knot of heat coiled low and tight in Call's body.

Damn, he thought. Haven *was* a woman, a lovely, desirable woman. It was foolish to think he could ignore that fact—maddening but definitely foolish. He'd never had a problem separating the person from the situation before. Never. It was, of course, due to his skills becoming rusty in the past two years, but unless remedied, it was going to make the whole assignment more difficult.

Control, Shannon, he ordered himself. Get it together. Now.

"Let's dig in before all this is cold," he said.

Haven placed some fries on Paige's tray, and the baby immediately snatched up some in each hand, bringing both fistfuls to her mouth.

Call chuckled as he watched the baby.

"Now, that's what I call enthusiasm for food," he said. "Your Paige is a girl after my own heart."

Haven's head snapped around, and she stared at Call.

Good night, Call's low, rumbling laugh had been one of the sexiest sounds she'd ever heard. It had been pure, unadulterated male, and had had a sensual impact on the part of her that was pure, unadulterated female.

From the moment that Call Shannon had stepped into her cozy cottage, he had seemed to fill it to overflowing by his presence. He was the first man to move within the expanse of her home, the first to sit across from her at that table. The heat that was swirling deep within her was increasing with every second and with every beat of her racing heart.

Oh, yes, she wanted Call Shannon.

And, oh, yes, he was very, *very* dangerous.

Haven got quickly to her feet, mumbling about needing a knife to cut up the hamburger for Paige, and a cup to give the baby some of the thick milk shake.

Call watched Haven rush into the kitchen, reaffirming in his mind that she was extremely nervous. His eyes swept over as much of the living room that was within his view.

Nothing fancy, he mused. The decor was mismatched, the furniture was a tad faded, a bit worn. There were toys scattered on the carpeted floor, and a playpen took up a chunk of space. But despite the clutter, it was obviously spit shined clean, and there was a lived-in homeyness about it.

A man could relax here, put his feet up, unwind from a hectic day. The aroma of dinner being cooked would waft through the air, and Paige's happy chatter and laughter would tinkle like wind chimes. Nice. Very nice. Later, after the baby was asleep for the night, he'd reach for Haven, pull her close, and...

Call cleared his throat and a frown settled over his features as he once again was assaulted by coiling heat low in his body. He snatched up his hamburger and took a big bite.

Haven sat back down at the table and busied herself preparing a bite-size dinner for Paige. She then began to eat her own meal, giving it her full attention and *not* looking at Call.

"Haven," Call finally said.

She jumped in her chair at the sudden sound of his voice.

"Yes?" she said, meeting his gaze.

"I'm not the big, bad wolf," he said quietly, "who's going to gobble you up. There's no reason for you to be so jumpy, so nervous."

Anger flashed in Haven's blue eyes. "Isn't there? You appear out of nowhere, and announce that you are—were—a longtime friend of Brian Larson's. You refuse to respect my wishes, my request that you exit my life as quickly as you'd entered it. You don't ask—you dictate—the fact that we're going to discuss Brian, whether I want to or not. So, fine. Let's talk about your old buddy Brian. We'll just chatter our little hearts out, then you're going to leave. Is that clear?''

Call continued to look at her for a long moment; then he tilted the chair back onto two legs and folded his arms loosely over his chest. A slow smile tugged at the corners of his mouth and widened into a grin.

"When you get that temper of yours in a rip," he said, "you do a bang-up job of it, darlin'."

Haven leaned toward him. "I am *not* your darlin', Mr. Shannon."

"Figure of speech."

"Erase it from your vocabulary when you're speaking to me."

He laughed and thudded the chair back onto four legs. "Yes, ma'am."

"And quit smiling," she said, none-too-quietly. She paused and shook her head. "Why am I yelling?" she said, throwing up her hands. "I don't yell. Well, I rarely yell. Look, Mr. Shannon..."

"Call," he said, his smile disappearing. "It's Call, Haven."

"Yes, well, Call, just what exactly did you want to discuss about Brian?"

He shrugged. "Whatever. I was really surprised to learn that he had a wife. The Brian I knew was definitely not the type of man inclined to marry anyone."

Haven averted her eyes from Call's. She ate two fries, then dabbed at Paige's mouth with a napkin before she spoke again.

"Well, he did marry someone. Me."

"Obviously. I can't understand why he didn't tell me about you." Call glanced at Paige, then redirected his attention to Haven. "Not only that, but he didn't share the news that he was going to become a father."

Haven met his gaze again, lifting her chin to a determined tilt.

"Brian didn't know about Paige. That is, he wasn't aware that I was pregnant. I never had a chance to tell him before he died."

Before I blew him away, Call thought. *Before I pulled the trigger on that gun and shot him.*

"I see," he said slowly. "I understand that Brian was killed in a hunting accident, one of those tragic, freak things that should never have happened."

"Yes. A man, hunting friend of his, came and told me. That man—I don't even remember his name— said he'd take care of all the arrangements. I was very young, Call, and didn't argue the point. I was told where to be for the memorial service, and once there, discovered that Brian's body had been cremated. It's all a blur in my mind."

"Haven," Call said, narrowing his eyes slightly, "Brian didn't hunt. It was one of those topics that he had very strong feelings about. He found no pleasure in tracking down and shooting defenseless animals." He had no qualms about shooting human beings, none at all, but wouldn't raise a weapon against an animal. "Why would he have been out hunting?"

Haven frowned. "I have no idea. I didn't even know he was on a hunting trip until the man came to tell me that Brian had been killed. Call, you have to understand that Brian and I had very little time together. I wasn't aware of all of his likes and dislikes."

"Well, you had to have known him well enough to have fallen in love with him and married him. Right?"

"I was married to Brian," she said, nodding. "However, it was over so quickly that, if it wasn't for my precious Paige, it would seem as though it never took place. I really didn't know all the little details about Brian Larson."

And she'd avoided saying that she'd loved him, Call mused. He'd bet his last ten bucks that she hadn't been in love with Brian. It was a deal, a marriage of convenience—he was convinced of that.

For what purpose? he wondered. There was a connection between the timing of Haven's brother getting off scot-free in regard to the robbery charges he had faced. That was now a given. Haven agreed to marry Brian in exchange for her brother's freedom.

But what else had she agreed to? Brian had been smart, cunning; he never did anything without a definite purpose.

Had Haven been a foreign agent before meeting Brian? Had he blown her cover and used bribery of her brother's freedom, then blackmail, to create a backup list of agents' names?

Was Haven innocent? Had she been forced to cooperate in hiding the list?

Did she even have the list? Was it in her possession without her realizing it? If that were true, or even if it weren't but foreign agents believed it to be, then she was in extreme danger.

And so was Paige.

Ah, damn, Call thought, an innocent baby's life could be at risk. The memories that fact evoked were as painful as a knife twisting in his gut. The darkness of the past held the ghosts of death, so many ghosts that haunted him.

He had to concentrate on the present, the assignment he'd agreed to take on in a vulnerable moment. That assignment was priority one, and had so many loose ends, so many questions.

It was up to him to unravel the puzzle and find the answers.

It was up to him to discover the truth about Haven Larson.

Five

The meal was finished in silence, except for Haven's motherly comments to Paige and the baby's answering chatter. When the entire contents of the sacks had been eaten, Haven whisked Paige from the high chair, announcing that the baby needed a dry diaper.

Call watched Haven as she hurried across the living room and disappeared into one of the bedrooms beyond. With a frown knitting his dark brows, he gathered the strewn papers and containers and stuffed the debris into the sacks.

He found a plastic-lined wastebasket beneath the kitchen sink, deposited the litter, then wandered back into the living room. Again his gaze swept over the room and again he felt its welcoming warmth and homeyness.

His living room in the ranch house at the Triple S, he mused, was four times this size. But it was just a big room, expensively decorated with furniture that had been in place when he'd bought the ranch. He rarely sat in that area, preferring his somewhat cluttered office that at least had an atmosphere of being lived in.

Call's gaze fell on a cloth doll that lay among the scattered toys on the floor. He settled on the edge of the sofa and reached for the doll, resting his elbows on his knees as he held the eight-inch toy in his hands.

The doll was made of bleached muslin and had a perpetual smile on her face that had been embroidered with brightly colored thread. Her hair was a tangled mass of brown yarn, and the wrinkled blue dress she wore had a red pocket that was half on, half off. One arm was slightly shorter than the other, and neat stitches gave evidence to the fact that said arm had been torn off, then resewn into place.

A smile tugged at the corners of Call's mouth.

"Well, little lady," he said quietly, "you look as though you've fought in a battle or two." He paused. "Or maybe you've just been given a helluva lot of mighty fine hugs."

Haven stood in the shadows at the edge of the room and stared at Call, hearing his softly spoken words. Her stomach did a strange flip-flop, and warm flutters seemed to dance around her heart.

Call Shannon, she mused, was a strong, strapping cowboy, a masculinity-personified man, who would demand respect just by walking into a room. He exuded confidence, with a tad of cocky arrogance thrown in for good measure. There was an aura of aloofness about him that would cause men to think twice about invading his space, and challenge some women to attempt to be the one who could get close to him.

Yet she was seeing another, very unexpected side to him, a gentleness, a near-vulnerability that was showing itself in the form of his large hands cradling a love-worn doll while he spoke to it as though it were human.

This Call Shannon did not qualify somehow to have been Brian Larson's best friend. If there had been a compassionate part to Brian's cold and calculating nature, she had never witnessed it. Call had a sensitivity that had prompted him to seek her out once he knew of her existence so they could talk of the man now dead.

She had to respect that. The fact that she wished to never even think about Brian would have to be set aside for now. If she was careful, did not glaringly reveal that she knew so little about Brian, she could satisfy Call's needs and send him on his way.

But, she knew, after Call was gone, the memory of him, though their encounter had been brief, would be slow to fade. He'd had a sensual impact on her like nothing she'd experienced before. It was frightening, yet in a secret, totally feminine section of her being, it was also exciting. That part she most definitely would ignore.

Haven took a deep breath, let it out slowly and crossed the room.

"That's Susie, Paige's favorite toy," she said, looking at the doll he still held. "It's a bit worse for wear. I made it out of material scraps, and she loved it from the minute she saw it."

Call nodded, then set the doll on the coffee table. Haven sat in a straight-backed chair on the opposite side of the table, and their gazes met.

Heat rocketed through Call's body, coiling tight and low. He registered a flash of anger toward Haven for her ability to push his sexual buttons, something he could not remember ever happening before. *He* was in control of his mind and body, moved toward a woman or away, depending on what *he* decided.

For an unexplainable and extremely irritating reason, Haven Larson possessed the ability to jar him, unsettle him, knock him off kilter. And the really damnable part was that she wasn't trying to do it. He'd been around the block enough times to know when a woman was on the make, and Haven simply wasn't. She was just being herself, and he was responding like an oversexed teenager.

His anger, he admitted to himself, was misplaced. He should be directing his fury at himself, not Haven. She wasn't guilty of purposely doing anything to evoke the reaction he was having to her. No, she was not guilty.

Not guilty, his mind echoed. *Haven Larson was not guilty.* She was an innocent victim of the workings of Brian Larson's evil and calculating mind. She was a pawn in a dangerous game being played out around her without her knowledge. *She was not guilty.*

Damn it, he was losing his objectivity again, thinking like a rookie agent instead of a seasoned professional. Being rusty was no excuse for conclusions drawn from an emotional base rather than from one built on hard facts.

Call leaned back and stretched his arms along the top of the sofa, hoping he was projecting a relaxed, casual attitude. In actuality, he was wired, tense, aware that every muscle in his body was tightened.

"Where's Paige?" he said.

"She's playing with blocks in her room. I imagine she'll wander out here in a few minutes."

"She ate her dinner with both hands. Have you noticed any inclination that she's going to be left-handed?"

"Left-handed?" Haven repeated. "No, she seems to be comfortable using either hand at this age. Why do you ask?"

He lifted one shoulder in a shrug. "It's no big deal. I just wondered, because Brian was left-handed."

Haven frantically searched her mind for a memory, a mental picture, of Brian eating or writing with his left hand, but came up blank. She could barely remember what he looked like, let alone zero in on a minute detail such as whether or not he was left- or right-handed.

Fake it, Haven, she ordered herself. She had to bluff her way through this.

"Oh, well, yes, of course, Brian was left-handed," she said, managing a small smile. "It will be interesting to see if Paige inherited that trait from him."

"Mmm," Call said, nodding.

Wrong, Haven, he thought. Nice try, but no cigar. Brian Larson had *not* been left-handed. There was no way in hell that Haven had been in love with Brian, swept off her feet in a romantic blur. Theirs had been a marriage of convenience used to free her delinquent brother. That point had now been checked and re-checked, and was at least one solid, proven fact.

But what had Brian asked of Haven in return? On that issue, Call was still at square one.

Haven glanced at the tattered cloth doll on the coffee table, then looked at Call again.

Maybe, she thought, just maybe, she could steer the conversation away from the subject of Brian. People liked to talk about themselves, and Call Shannon was probably not an exception to the rule.

She knew she wasn't doing well in her attempt to casually discuss Brian. She hadn't even known he was left-handed, for heaven's sake. Whether or not Call found her lack of knowledge odd, she didn't know. But, dear Lord, when he held her immobile with those dark eyes of his, she felt as though he could see the secrets of her soul.

"Do you have a family, Call?" she asked, striving for a calm, pleasant tone of voice.

"No."

"Oh. Well, I thought perhaps you did, because you didn't appear startled when Paige latched on to your leg, or when she called you Da-da. It just occurred to me that you might be a father who is accustomed to being around a toddler."

"No."

"Goodness, Call," she said dryly, "do you have to blather on and on like that? I mean, with a little practice you could probably get the hang of giving nice, crisp, short answers to questions."

Call smiled. "Sorry. I'm not into idle chitchat, I guess. If one word says it instead of ten, then I use one word. I get high marks in listening, though."

He got high marks in a lot of areas, she thought, but she refused to start clicking off the list of his physical attributes again. She was also ignoring the ridiculous elation she'd felt when he'd implied that he wasn't married.

Furthermore, she was paying no attention whatsoever to the shimmer of heat that had swept through her when Call had smiled that devastating smile of his. Oh, how she wished this evening would end, allowing her to escape from the haunting memories of Brian and from her disturbing reactions to Call.

Paige toddled into the room, dragging a faded pink blanket, the thumb of her other hand planted in her mouth. She went to Haven and laid her head on her mother's knee. Haven scooped her onto her lap and kissed the baby's forehead.

"Hello, sleepy girl," she said. "It's a quick bath, then into bed with you, miss." Perfect. That had been a subtle message to Call to haul himself out of there. "Well," she said, getting to her feet with Paige in her arms, "as you can see, I have to get Paige ready for bed now. So, I guess..."

"Go right ahead," he said. "Take your time. I'll just flip through one of the magazines there on the coffee table until you're finished."

"But..." she started, then mentally threw up her hands in defeat. "Fine." She hurried from the room.

Call got to his feet and began to stroll around the small, cluttered room, giving the appearance of idle interest as he studied pictures on the walls and books in the bookcase. If Haven observed him, she'd see a man who was passing the time until she returned.

What he was actually doing was mentally cataloging what was there. He would later draw a detailed picture of what he was now memorizing. He would then know, upon a future visit to Haven's, if anything was missing, plus be able to study the drawing for the multitude of places where a list might be concealed.

It was a start, which was all he could accomplish at that point. He couldn't exactly ask Haven for a tour of her bedroom.

Haven's bedroom, his mind taunted. It was probably decorated in a frilly and feminine motif, with ruffles and a slew of lacy pillows on the bed. Why women cluttered up a perfectly good bed with bunches of extra, worthless, little pillows, he'd never know. But then, he'd never claimed to be able to understand the workings of a woman's mind.

Women were complicated creatures, no doubt about it. From the beginning of time, a hundred-pound woman could cut a two-hundred-pound man off at the knees, rendering him virtually helpless.

Other men, he told himself. Not him. So, okay, he didn't really understand women, but neither did he fall prey to them. Haven had jarred him, pushed his sexual buttons, but he'd straightened all that out in his mind.

Haven's bedroom, his brain echoed, as his thoughts skittered back to the subject. Haven *in* her bedroom, closing out the world as she welcomed him into her embrace. They'd make slow, sweet love for hours in unhurried pleasure, kissing, caressing, discovering, then meshing their bodies into one entity, and reaching heights of ecstasy that he knew, just somehow knew, would be like nothing he'd experienced before.

God, how he wanted her.

But, damn it, that want, that burning, aching want within him, was going to get in his way, make it difficult, if not impossible, for him to carry out his assignment to its proper end.

"Da-da."

Call spun around at the sound of Paige's voice, and nearly groaned aloud at the exquisite picture before him. Haven was holding a pajama-clad Paige, who had rosy cheeks from the warmth of her bath, and damp curls that framed her face, which was a tiny, mirror image of Haven's.

Haven was looking at her daughter, the smile on her face so loving, so serene, so incredibly beautiful, it caused his heart to thunder.

But then, suddenly, he felt as though he'd been punched in the gut. A swirling dark cloud seemed to be weaving around him, crushing him, making it difficult to breathe. The dark entity hammered its identity against his mind with a unrelenting cadence; its name was loneliness.

Haven and Paige stood only the distance of a small room away, yet to Call they were a world apart. They were sunshine to his darkness, innocence to his stark knowledge of the evils beyond the door. They were woman and child, needing only the man to complete the family unit.

And Call Shannon knew, as he stood alone, as the darkness consumed him and gripped his heart and soul with a tight, cold fist, that because of who he'd been, what he'd done, where he'd walked, that he could never be the man in the circle of sunshine that was Haven and Paige.

"There's Susie," Haven said, bringing Call from his tormenting thoughts. "There's your baby, Paige." She crossed the room and picked up the cloth doll from the coffee table. "Here you go."

Paige reached out, took the doll, then planted a smacking kiss on the cloth face.

"What a nice kiss, sweetheart," Haven said, laughing. "Susie may need to see a chiropractor, but the thought was there."

Haven glanced at Call where he stood across the room, her smile changing instantly to a frown.

There was no readable expression on his face, no clue as to what he was thinking. Yet, there was *something,* an undefinable something, emanating from him like an invisible energy source crackling through the air.

Shadows were cast over him by the lamp on the end table, making him appear even bigger, more massive, his strength and masculinity more pronounced in the semidarkness.

A flicker of fear caused her to tighten her hold on Paige, but the sensation vanished in the next instant.

No, she thought, she wasn't afraid of Call on a physical plane. Perhaps she should be, because she'd invited him into her home without really knowing him. She would be powerless to defend herself against him if he was intent on doing her bodily harm.

But it wasn't fear she was registering, it was a sense of safety, of knowing for the first time in her entire life that there was a presence of strength standing between her and Paige and anyone who might threaten them.

Such nonsense, Haven, she admonished herself. Now she was declaring Call Shannon to be her knight in shining armor. What foolishness was next? She'd be Cinderella, and Call would be Prince Charming? She definitely did *not* behave in a normal manner when in close proximity to Call. Enough, Haven Larson, was enough.

"Say good night to Call, Paige," she said, forcing a lightness to her voice. "Say 'night-night.'"

"Ni, ni," the baby said. "Da-da, ni, ni."

"Good night, kiddo," Call said quietly.

"I'll be right back," Haven said.

She turned and left the room, talking to Paige about sweet dreams and the fact that Mommy would be home with her for the next two days.

Call watched them go, then dragged both hands down his face as a weary-sounding sigh escaped from his lips.

Lord, he fumed, thoughts were bouncing back and forth in his mind like Ping-Pong balls. One minute he was performing as a trained agent—alert, on guard, watching for clues to give him answers to Haven's innocence or guilt.

Then she'd reappear and he became nothing more than a man reacting to the lure of a lovely woman. His protective instincts rose to the fore, Haven's total innocence was a given and he was fiercely determined to ensure her and Paige's safety.

He was, in short, a wreck, a mental mess.

"All tucked in," Haven said, coming back into the room. "Would you care for something to drink, Call?"

"No, thank you."

She settled again into the straight-backed chair, and looked at him questioningly as he remained standing where he was.

"Haven," he said, "you mentioned that during the short time you had with Brian, he was very busy, involved in what you called a complicated project. What exactly was he doing?"

"Well, he was..." she started, frantically searching her mind for what to say. What had Brian been involved in? She really didn't know. "He was coordinating a government project. He worked for the government. Oh, well, I guess you know that because you were close friends. He really didn't share any details about it."

"I see. You'd think a man would talk to his wife about his work, wouldn't you?"

"I don't know about men in general, but Brian didn't discuss his job with me. He simply said he did special projects for the government." She paused. "He did say that I would be helping him with something in the near future, but I never knew what it was. He died before he explained what I was to do."

Bingo, Call thought. Brian had been setting it up, getting ready to give Haven the list. Or had he actually given it to her without her realizing it? An even better question was why he was automatically believing what Haven had just said. The Ping-Pong balls were going nuts again.

"Ah, hell," Call said, staring up at the ceiling for a few seconds.

"What's wrong? You seem ... I don't know, angry, or frustrated, or..." She shook her head.

Tell her, Call's mind yelled. Tell her that Brian was a traitor to his country, and that fact was now possibly placing her and Paige in harm's way.

Tell her. Tell her that nothing, *nothing,* was going to happen to her or her baby. Anyone with an intention of hurting her would have to get past him, and that wasn't going to happen.

Tell her. Tell her that he had pulled the trigger on the gun that had killed Brian Larson.

Damn it, Shannon, tell her.

"Call? What is it?"

He looked at her for a long moment before speaking.

"Nothing. Nothing is wrong, Haven." He cleared his throat. "Well, I'd better shove off. I appreciate your talking to me about Brian. I hope it didn't upset you to drag up old memories."

Haven got to her feet. "No, I'm fine. Thank you for the dinner. It was a real treat to have fast food. I'll eat my veggies every day next week to make up for it."

"There you go," he said, attempting a smile that failed to materialize.

He crossed the room and retrieved his Stetson from the chair at the table, as Haven went to the door. He met her there and settled the hat on his head.

"Haven," he said, looking directly into her eyes, "how would you and Paige like to spend the day at my ranch tomorrow?"

"Oh, I don't think—"

"It will be a new experience for Paige. You're supposed to do that, you know—make sure little kids have new experiences. I'll pick you up around nine."

"I have chores that—"

Call silenced her by giving her a quick kiss on the lips.

"Nine o'clock. Good night, darlin'."

Call left, closing the door behind him with a quiet click. Haven pressed her fingertips to her tingling lips, the lingering heat from Call's kiss traveling through her.

"I'm not your darlin'," she said, hearing the trembling in her voice.

Six

Call strode across the kitchen with Lupe scurrying behind him, having to take two steps to his one.

"I'll make very nice lunch," Lupe said, to Call's broad back. "*Sí*, yes, *mucho* delicious lunch for your special lady."

Call stopped dead in his tracks, causing Lupe to bump into him with a startled "oomph." He turned and glowered down at her.

"Lupe, I'm going to say this once more," he said, obviously straining for patience. "Haven is *not* my lady. Have you got that?"

"No," Lupe said, crossing her arms firmly over her ample bosom. "You've never brought a woman here before. Not one time. So, this Haven is special. Is she a lady, or a tarnished woman from the streets?"

"Of course she's a lady," Call said, volume on high.

Lupe beamed. "Then I'm right on the dollar. Haven is your special lady."

"Money," Call said. "It's 'right on the money.'" He paused. "Damn it, quit pulling me off track. Haven is not—"

"Shoo, shoo," Lupe said, flapping her hands at him. "You're to be late if you don't leave now. Go get your special lady, and the little one. Oh, my, a baby on the Triple S." She sighed wistfully. "This is truly a blue-letter day."

"Red-letter day," Call bellowed.

"*Sí*. Yes. I'm happy you finally admit it. Go get your special lady and baby Paige."

"Oh, man," Call said, through clenched teeth. He snatched his black Stetson off a long, wooden hat rack mounted on the wall, and jammed it onto his head. "I might as well be talking to a tree. Goodbye, Lupe."

"Goodbye, Call," she said, ever so sweetly. She continued to smile, ignoring the fact that Call had slammed the door so hard, the dishes on the table had rattled. A moment later she frowned. "A tree?"

Outside, Call was intercepted by José. The man was in his early fifties like his wife, and was as reed slim as she was plump. His skin was tawny from heritage, but had the leathery appearance that comes from spending many years working in the sun.

"Headin' into Houston now?" José asked.

"Yeah. José, your wife is going to be the death of me yet."

José's eyes widened. "Lupe threatened to shoot you?"

Call chuckled in spite of himself. He took off his Stetson, flicked a speck of dust from the brim, then settled it back on his head.

"No," he said, "Lupe isn't going to shoot me. Well, I don't think she is. Is everything under control here?"

"*Sí.* The boys will move that one bunch of cattle to the north range like you said." José paused, looked into the distance for a long moment, then redirected his attention to Call. "You won't be back 'til lunch?"

Call frowned slightly. "No. Is there something you want to talk to me about before I go?"

"No, no," José said quickly. He slid his hands into his jeans pockets and rocked slowly back and forth on the balls of his feet. "I was just checking double."

"Double-checking," Call said absently, as he continued to look intently at José.

"Right," José said, staring at the toes of his boots. "See ya later, Call."

"Yeah," he said, then turned and walked slowly away.

He glanced over his shoulder at José, but the older man was already hurrying toward the barn. Call slid behind the wheel of a station wagon that had seen better days, and minutes later was driving away from the ranch.

José, he mused, had been acting strangely, very weird. He'd never seen his foreman so jumpy, nervous. The man was usually laid-back and easygoing to the point that his intelligence and common sense really weren't apparent to someone meeting him for the first time.

But this morning? José was edgy, wired—and even more disturbing was the fact that he hadn't looked directly at Call, wouldn't meet his eyes as they spoke.

Call's frown deepened, and he drummed his fingers on the steering wheel as he drove along the deserted road. He glanced automatically in the rearview and side mirrors, doing so without moving his head. If anyone was following him, he would not appear to be checking for their presence. He did it by rote, born of years of his survival being contingent upon his constant awareness of what was going on around him.

Today he was oblivious to the lush, green acres and the grazing cattle. He didn't see the clear blue sky and fluffy puffs of clouds, nor the pristine-white wooden fence that surrounded the land that he could proudly call his own.

Ease up, Shannon, he finally told himself. He was overreacting to an incident that had no significance, didn't mean a thing. He was reading far, far too much into José's uncharacteristic behavior.

That was due, Call reasoned, to the fact that he had taken his instincts, reflexes, the sixth sense—that went along with being a top-notch agent—out of cold storage. He was chipping away the rust, and dusting off the cobwebs. In doing that, he was on red alert about every little thing—ridiculously so.

Okay, he thought, with a decisive nod. He'd figured that out. No problem. He was shifting gears to where his mind was *supposed* to be: concentrating on Haven Larson.

Haven, his mind echoed. He'd dreamed about her. He'd pushed that disturbing fact into a shadowy corner of his brain shortly after awakening.

Granted, in the past he'd had dreams about the assignment he was then working on. Where his conscious mind left off as he drifted to sleep, his subconscious picked up and continued to deal with the issue at hand. The dreams were often distorted, a maze of interwoven images and actions centered on the adversary he was concentrating on.

But the dreams of Haven had been far different. He knew it and was none too happy as he fully acknowledged that fact. There had been no visions of Brian, nor clouded faces of the agents put in jeopardy because of the list. There had been no tiring chases through the darkness, nor glimpses of any weapons.

The dreams had been of Haven, just Haven. They were sensual dreams with Haven emerging from a misty fog, smiling, wearing a sheer white gown that fell to the tops of her bare feet. The material had swirled around her in graceful folds, teasing, hinting at what lay beneath but not fully revealing her slender body to his smoldering gaze.

She had beckoned to him, holding out her arms, her delicate hands reaching for him. Each time he moved forward, the fog thickened, clearing moments later to show Haven farther back, beyond his grasp. She had whispered his name over and over, her voice thrumming with passion. He'd answered, telling her he was there, wanting her.

Again and again, the scene was repeated, with Call never able to reach her, encircle her with his arms, nestle her to his aching body.

He'd awakened with a start at dawn's light, drenched in sweat, his heart pounding. Even now, driving along the quiet road, the lifelike images from the dreams flitted in his mind's eye, causing intense heat to coil low and tight within him.

As the remembrance of the brief but enticing kiss shared with Haven began to creep in around the edges of his mind, he swore under his breath. He shifted slightly on the seat, willing his body back under his command.

This, he decided, letting out a pent-up breath, was going to be a very long day.

Haven sat on the sofa, then was up again in the next instant, wandering restlessly around the cluttered living room.

She did *not* want to spend the day with Call Shannon at his ranch.

The night had been a seemingly endless stretch of hours during which she'd tossed and turned, dozed, then repeated the process. The firm directives she'd issued to herself to push Call far, far from her mind were ignored. He was there, close, towering above her, sometimes smiling, later frowning, then often looking at her intently, just looking, with those damnable dark eyes of his.

The bright sunshine of day had not chased the image of Call away. He'd followed her into the shower, and now seemed to be filling her small living room to overflowing.

Why? she asked herself for the umpteenth time. Why had she agreed to this outing?

She stopped her aimless trek and narrowed her eyes.

She *hadn't* agreed to this outing. Her objections had been silenced by Call's kiss. The nerve of that man to kiss her out of the blue, just step up and kiss her, as though he had every right to do so. Oh, he was a cocky, arrogant so-and-so, and...

And that brief kiss had ignited a fire of desire within her that was still a glowing ember.

"Oh, that despicable man," she said aloud, planting her fists on her hips.

She wasn't going to his ranch. She wasn't some starry-eyed adolescent who lost the ability to think when close to a devastatingly handsome, masculinity-personified man.

Call had caught her off guard with his unexpected kiss—dear heaven, what a kiss—and then he'd escaped through the door before she could function again and flatly refuse his invitation to the ranch.

Well, she had news for that cowboy. She wasn't budging from her cottage.

A sharp knock sounded at the door, and Haven jumped in surprise. She placed one hand on her racing heart, took a deep breath, let it out slowly, then marched to the door. She flung it open with every intention of informing Call Shannon that she wasn't going anywhere with him.

But as her eyes met Call's, all rational thought fled. She vaguely realized that he was wearing boots, jeans, a steel-gray Western shirt and a black Stetson, but beyond that she completely forgot what it was she'd planned to say.

"Hello, Haven," Call said. Nice. Haven in snug jeans and a red cotton blouse was very, *very* nice.

His voice was low and rumbly, causing a frisson of heat to dance through her. The memory of the exquisite sensation of his lips capturing hers caused a warm flush on her cheeks.

Oh, good heavens, she thought, giving herself a mental shake, how long had she been standing there gawking at him?

"Come in, Call," she said, tearing her gaze from his. She stepped back to allow him to enter, then closed the door behind him.

"Hi, kiddo," Call said to Paige, as the baby toddled into the room.

"Da-da," Paige said, smiling.

"There you go," he said.

"Call," Haven said, "I didn't realize how much equipment it would require to be able to take Paige to spend the day at your ranch. There's an overstuffed diaper bag, the playpen so she can nap, the car seat has to be shifted from my vehicle and... Well, I thought you might want to reconsider your invitation."

Call frowned. "Toting Paige's things is no problem. There's plenty of room in the station wagon." He paused. "You make it sound as though you haven't taken her anywhere for the day before now."

"Well, I haven't. We go to the zoo, or the park, but we haven't ventured far. I've never left her with a sitter other than when I'm working, either."

"I see," he said slowly. "That's all very nice for Paige, your being constantly with her. But what about you, Haven? I can't believe that Brian would want you to live such a tight, narrow existence out of a sense of loyalty to him."

"I'm not doing it because of Brian," she said. Oh, darn, she'd revealed far too much by that retort. "What I mean," she said quickly, "is that I enjoy being with my baby. Being a mother is extremely important to me."

"I'm sure it is," he said, nodding, "but what about Haven Larson, the woman? Wouldn't you like to get dressed up and go out to dinner?" He shrugged. "Or the theater, or whatever?"

Yes, Haven's mind whispered. She'd love to have an evening out where she had no responsibility other than to thoroughly enjoy herself. She'd dine... not eat...dine at a ritzy restaurant, wearing a stunning dress. That in itself was a joke, because she didn't own a fancy dress. After dinner there'd be dancing to dreamy music. That was ridiculous, too, because she didn't know how to dance.

"Haven?"

"What? Oh, I was miles away. To answer your question, Call, no, I have no desire to do the town. I'd rather spend my time with Paige." She paused and frowned slightly. "I don't want to sound rude, but how I spend my private hours is really none of your business."

Call grinned, then pushed up his Stetson a bit with his thumb.

"Sure it is, darlin'," he said. "Now I know that I'll have to do some smooth talking to convince you to go out to dinner with me one of these nights."

"Oh, but—"

"Hey, there," he said, directing his attention to Paige. He hunkered down in front of the baby. "I see you have your favorite toy, Paige. Is that Susie?" He pointed to the cloth doll that Paige was holding upside down by one leg.

"Da-da," Paige said, swinging the doll in the air. "Susie, Susie, Susie." She grabbed the toy with both of her tiny hands and gave it a loud kiss somewhere in the vicinity of Susie's tummy. "Baby."

Call chuckled as he watched her, then his smile faded.

Such innocence, he mused. Paige's world was a sheltered cocoon containing love, security and sunshine. And there he was only a few feet away from her representing the dark side of life.

Paige Larson kept that beat-up doll close to her at all times because it was familiar, it was hers.

And Call Shannon? he asked himself. Oh, yeah, he had the familiar with him at that very moment, and it was his, like it or not. There was a .38 revolver in an ankle holster inside his right boot.

He planted his hands on his thighs, and leveled himself up, turning to look at Haven. She met his gaze.

"You're very good with children," she said. "As big as you are, you might be intimidating, but you went down to Paige's level so she could see you clearly."

He shrugged. "I didn't think about it, I just did it. She sure is a cute kid." He smiled. "Have you decided which fancy restaurant you want to go to on the night we do the town?"

Haven opened her mouth to tell him in no uncertain terms that she had no intention of going out to dinner with him. To her own surprise, the angry retort was forgotten as she burst into laughter.

"You're exhausting," she said, still smiling. "You're so cocky, it's a sin, yet you manage to get your own way more often than not. You are, Call Shannon, a very exasperating man."

"There you go," he said, tugging his Stetson lower. "You've got that all figured out. It'll save a lot of time if you don't fuss at me about things, don't get naggy."

"Just do as I'm told?" She laughed again and shook her head. "You're unbelievable."

"I don't know why. It makes perfect sense to me." He glanced around. "Well, darlin', let's get this show on the road."

"Yes, sir," Haven said, then rolled her eyes heavenward.

*   *   *

The lighthearted mood prevailed as they drove away from Haven's cottage with Paige in her car seat in the back seat. They chatted, one topic flowing into the next, covering books they'd read, the political scene, state of the economy, then on to Haven's questions regarding the workings of the Triple S. They finally left the heavy traffic of the city behind, and were soon driving along a dirt road.

"Triple S," Haven said. "The S is for Shannon, I imagine. Who are the other two Shannons?" She frowned as she saw a muscle jump along Call's suddenly tightened jaw. "I thought that was a reasonable question, but apparently it isn't."

Call glanced over at her, then redirected his attention to the road.

"It's reasonable," he said quietly, "but I'm going to pass on answering it right now."

"All right, Call," she said softly. She turned to check on Paige. "Sound asleep. Ever since she was a tiny baby, riding in a car has put her to sleep. She'd be loads of fun on a trip across the country."

Call chuckled. "A real ball of fire." He looked in the rearview mirror.

Damn, he thought. The dust he could see indicated that someone was behind them several miles back. Whoever it was had been there since they'd hit the dirt road. They could very well have been dogging them in the city traffic, too. If that was the case, they were good at tailing, very good, because he'd been on full alert for a tail since leaving Haven's.

He slowed his speed, then waited to see what the vehicle behind them would do.

The puff of dust came closer, then began to recede, putting the original distance between them.

Hell, Call thought, his grip on the steering wheel tightening. There was no doubt about it. They had company. MacIntosh had been right about the need for immediate action regarding the mess Brian had made. But then, Peter MacIntosh was rarely wrong.

Time to regroup, Call decided. He'd been moving fairly slowly, getting to know Haven, making her comfortable with him. It had been nice chatting with her, and he'd actually forgotten for minutes at a stretch that he was in the middle of an important assignment, something he'd never done while an active agent.

That dust behind them said he'd have to speed things up, wing it, play it as it came. Damn.

"Call?" Haven said. "Is something wrong? You seem so tense all of a sudden."

"Yeah," he said, a cold edge to his voice, "something is wrong. Let's start at the top, Haven."

"I don't know what you mean."

"Don't you? Then try this on for size. Brian Larson was *not* left-handed."

Seven

Haven's eyes widened in shock, and she could actually feel the color draining from her face. Chilling fear swept through her.

Her eyes darted to Paige, who still slept soundly, and she had to force herself not to reach over the seat and snatch the baby up and into the safety of her arms. She tore her gaze from her daughter, and looked at Call.

"Who are you?" she said, hearing the trembling in her voice. "What do you want?"

Ah, damn, Call thought, a painful knot tightening in his gut. Listen to her. She was terrified, scared to death of *him*. He'd purposely spoken to her in a cold, menacing voice in order to jolt her into revealing to him what he needed to know.

But *he* wasn't the enemy. *He* wasn't the one she had to be afraid of. He was going to protect her and Paige, place himself between them and whoever was in the vehicle following them.

This time, by God, the woman and child he'd vowed to watch over *would not die!*

Nothing was going to happen to Haven Larson or her baby. Nothing!

The question of Haven's innocence or guilt had not been answered, but that was not the issue now. What was important was her safety. She was a vulnerable woman with a child, a woman who had touched him in an emotional place deep within him that was foreign and new, and in a sensual way that caused him to continually lose the strict command he held over his own body.

She was Haven.

And for now, that was it, pure and simple, bottom line.

The complexities of the assignment would take second seat until he was assured there was no longer any danger present from the occupants of the car following them.

But he needed information, he mentally argued. He was flying blind, drawing conclusions on his own that had to be verified by Haven. The existence of the vehicle behind them said he had to push Haven for facts.

Yes, at the moment her welfare came first, but he'd have to continue to press without scaring her to death.

"Damn you," Haven said, jarring Call from his thoughts, "talk to me. Where are you taking me? What do you want, Call Shannon? Or is that even your real name?"

He glanced over at her, the knot tightening as he saw her pale face and the fear in her blue eyes. He looked quickly in the mirrors, and saw the cloud of dust in the distance. Swearing under his breath, he redirected his attention to the road.

"Haven," he said quietly, a gentle tone to his voice, "I'm sorry. I didn't mean to frighten you. I *am* Call Shannon, we're going to my ranch, the Triple S, and I did grow up with Brian Larson. But there's more to it than that."

He paused, searching his mind for the proper words, a way to explain the sordid story without frightening Haven even more.

"I would have waited until we got to the ranch to talk to you about…" He started, then shook his head. "But we've run out of time."

"Time for what? You're talking in riddles." Haven attempted to force strength into her voice, hoping that it would materialize. "I want straight answers, Call. Now. Right now."

"Haven, we're being followed."

Her head snapped around and she looked out the rear window of the station wagon.

"Dear heaven," she whispered. "Why?"

"Did you cut a deal with Brian Larson? Did you agree to marry him, although you hardly knew him, in exchange for the charges against your brother being dropped?"

No! her mind screamed. Oh, please, no. She'd worked so hard to overcome the shame, to put to rest the haunting, taunting ghosts of the past. She'd struggled to free herself from what had gone before, and she'd won. And now? Call was dragging her back to the dark, chilling place, demanding that she remember.

"Why are you doing this to me?" she said, unwelcomed tears brimming her eyes.

"I have no choice. Brian was an agent for the government, working out of a special agency that the general public knows nothing about. I was one of those agents, too, until I quit two years ago."

"Dear Lord," she said, shaking her head, "this is like a bad movie." An errant tear spilled onto her cheek, and she swept it away with a jerky motion. "Secret agents?"

"Yes." Call paused, and let out a deep breath. "Haven, answer the question. Did you marry Brian in exchange for your brother's freedom? I believe that you did."

"You can believe anything you choose," she said, her voice rising. "I was young, inexperienced, hadn't had a normal childhood. I didn't have high school dates, go to parties and proms. Brian was handsome, charming, promised me a world I could only fantasize about. Did I cut a deal? Marry Brian to free my brother? I married Brian to become his wife, and now I'm his widow. That's all I have to say to you, Call Shannon."

"Damn it, would you trust me a little here? I need the truth, Haven."

"Trust you? As of a few minutes ago, I don't even know you. Leave me alone. Just leave me alone, Call."

Call glanced in the rearview mirror and his jaw tightened into a hard line. In the next instant he whipped the car onto a narrow side road that was like a shadowy tunnel due to the large trees edging the path. He gunned the motor and the vehicle leapt forward, bouncing along the rutted road.

Haven looked anxiously at Paige. The baby stirred, but didn't awaken. Haven shifted in her seat, one hand braced against the dashboard as she looked directly at Call.

"Where are you going?" she said, an echo of tears still in her voice.

"I've got to lose this joker," he said, narrowing his eyes. "I want him, believe me, I want him, but not while I'm with you and Paige." A pulse beat wildly in his temple and a muscle ticked in his jaw. "I swear to you, Haven, *nothing* is going to happen to you or your baby. Anyone trying to get to you will have to go through me, and that won't be an easy trip."

Haven stared at him, waiting for another rush of fear to wash over her, clutching at her with icy fingers. But it didn't come. Instead, a warmth suffused her, swirling around her heart, touching her soul.

She was frightened, confused, beleaguered by an amalgam of other emotions that were tangled into a jumbled maze in her mind. Yet, there, deep within her, gaining strength with every beat of her pounding heart, was the warmth that brought with it a strange calmness that soothed and quieted.

Because Call Shannon was there.

With words that held the biting coldness of a stark winter day, he had sworn to protect her and Paige.

And she believed him.

She trusted him to keep her safe from harm.

She was drawn to him on a physical plane with an intensity she'd never experienced before, but there was more, much more. Emotions were intertwined with the sensual yearnings. For the first time in her life, she felt an unexplainable connection—a bond—with a man.

But the trust she felt had its limits, its boundaries. Call was demanding to know her darkest secrets, wanted her to relive pain and shame beyond measure.

The truth would bring his censure and scorn. The truth spoken aloud would shatter the very essence of herself that she'd worked so hard to create, brick by emotional brick.

She couldn't give him that power. No. Her trust in him didn't reach that far, wasn't strong or deep enough.

Call suddenly brought the car to an abrupt halt, jarring Haven from her thoughts. She looked out the window and saw that they were parked behind a small, weather-beaten, wooden cabin. Call turned off the ignition and flung the car door open.

"Let's go," he said. "Inside. I'll get Paige, you bring that...whatever you called it...diaper bag thing if she's going to need what's in it."

Haven did as instructed, aware that icy fear was consuming her once again, causing a metallic taste in her mouth. Call unsnapped the seat belt holding the car seat, and lifted it and the baby out of the vehicle. Paige opened her eyes, blinked, then frowned.

Call jerked his head at Haven, indicating she should go ahead of him. She opened the cabin door and entered with Call right behind her.

"Close the door," he said. "There aren't any locks on this place, though."

He set the car seat in the center of a wooden table that had never been blessed with a coat of paint, then strode to one of the small, dusty front windows.

"Mama," Paige said, in a whining voice. "Mama."

Haven hurried to the baby, set the diaper bag on the table, then undid the straps that held Paige securely in place. She lifted the baby into her arms and held her so tightly, the toddler squirmed in protest. Haven kissed her on the forehead, and lightened her hold.

"Call?" Haven said, surprised at the strength and steadiness of her voice. "What's going on? Who's following us?" She glanced around. "Where are we? I mean, I realize this is a cabin in the woods, but... There's so much that I don't understand, and it's all so frightening."

Call turned his head for a moment to look at her, then his gaze swept over the interior of the rustic cabin. There was a small fireplace, a faded sofa and chair, two sagging cots along one wall, and a kitchen area with a wood-burning stove and a hand pump by a small, rusty sink. The wooden table on which he'd placed Paige's car seat was flanked by two wooden chairs painted a strange shade of green. He switched his eyes back to the window.

"This cabin," he said quietly, "isn't mine. It's just this side of the beginning of my property that starts around a curve in the road that is up ahead of where I turned off. I'm hoping our shadow will go on around the curve a ways before he realizes he's lost us. That road I turned on is easy to miss if you don't know it's there. A lot depends on how quickly the dust we kicked up settles."

"But who—" Haven started.

"Sit down on that sofa with Paige. Someone has used this place fairly recently. Everything has obviously been cleaned. It's not exactly spit shined, but it could be a lot worse."

Haven went to the sofa and sank onto one of the lumpy cushions, instantly realizing that it was a relief to sit due to her trembling legs.

"Call, please," she said, "tell me who's following us and why. I don't understand any of this."

"This situation is Brian Larson's legacy," he said, a rough edge to his voice.

"Mama," Paige said, wiggling on Haven's lap.

"Call, I need to get the diaper bag so I can change Paige, and give her some juice."

"Yeah, okay, but go right back to the sofa and stay there. I don't want you wandering around. If I tell you to get down on the floor, do it."

"Dear heaven," she whispered, getting to her feet.

She crossed the room, put Paige in the car seat, slid the handles of the diaper bag onto her arm, then hurried back to the sofa with her heavy, cumbersome cargo.

After spreading a small blanket on the sofa, she changed Paige's diaper, placed her in the car seat on the floor, and handed her a plastic baby bottle filled with apple juice. The baby gripped the bottle in both hands and merrily kicked her feet as she began to drink.

She had to get Paige off a bottle, Haven thought. She could drink from a cup, was beyond the stage of baby bottles. Paige would fuss, but it was time to break her of—Haven Larson, where is your mind? There she sat blissfully chattering to herself about child care when she should be addressing the fact that she was in the midst of a living nightmare. Maybe she was bordering on hysteria.

She shook her head, then looked at Call again. The tension and leashed power emanating from him was a nearly tangible entity.

Call and Brian had been secret agents, and because of Brian's involvement in the unnamed agency, someone was following her, someone Call obviously considered dangerous. Brian's legacy—that's what Call had said this horror was. What did he mean? What did *any* of this mean?

And what, she wondered dismally, would Call think of her if he knew what she had done? Why Call's opinion of her mattered so very much, she didn't know.

Oh, Haven, she admonished herself, grow up. She was grasping at straws, attempting to convince herself that she didn't yet know what Call's reaction to the truth would be. He would view her now as she, herself, had when she was forced to face what she had done: cheap, tawdry, not worthy of respect.

She closed her eyes for a moment, fighting against threatening tears. She drew a wobbly breath, then looked at Call.

"Call," she said quietly, aware that her voice was quivering, "I realize that you think I'm keeping the truth from you and you're angry, but please, please, Call, don't let that stand in your way of keeping my baby safe from harm. Paige is innocent of any wrongdoing and—"

Call's head snapped around and Haven's breath caught when she saw the fury visible on his face and in his dark eyes.

"Damn it, Haven, if you married Brian in exchange for your brother's freedom, do you think I'd condemn you for it? Not even close. You were pushed against the wall. You were young, frightened, alone. Brian played on that, used it for his own gain. You were a victim of circumstances, combined with a smooth-talking, very slick operator. Brian Larson was scum. He—forget it." He switched his attention back to the window.

"But I thought you two had been friends since your childhood."

"We were," he said, his voice low. "Very close friends, like brothers. People change, Haven."

"You didn't seek me out to relive fond memories of your times with Brian, did you?"

"No."

Haven shook her head. "It's all so confusing, so frightening. I don't understand any of this."

"You will. I'll explain it to you later. The first order of business is for us to get out of here."

He strode across the room, stopping in front of her. Haven got to her feet.

"Any plan I come up with to leave here," he said, "stinks." He looked down at Paige, who was carrying on a babbling, one-sided conversation with her now-empty bottle. He met Haven's troubled gaze again. "You've got to promise me that you'll do exactly as I tell you."

"Yes," she said, her voice unsteady, "yes, of course. I will. I trust you, Call."

He opened his mouth to speak, then closed it again, realizing that what he might have said was overshadowed and forgotten due to Haven's softly spoken words.

I trust you, Call.

Lord, he thought, what was the matter with him? He felt strange, disoriented, as if he'd suddenly been flung into a foreign place where he'd never gone before.

It seemed as though he'd been rescued from a cold, foggy haze and led to a space where warm sunshine prevailed, not having known until now how oppressive and chilling the fog had been.

I trust you, Call.

"Haven..." he said, not realizing he'd said her name aloud.

"I'm listening, Call. Tell me exactly what you want me to do."

Call blinked, then frowned, as he returned to reality with a thud. Haven trusted him to a point, he realized, but not enough to tell him the truth about her marriage to Brian. Not enough.

"All right," he said. "We're leaving. I want you and Paige on the floor of the back seat. Stay down, below the windows. No matter what happens, don't move until I say you can."

Haven drew a steadying breath, then squared her shoulders.

"I understand."

"I know you're frightened, Haven, but you're doing great, really terrific. Let's go."

Minutes later, Haven and Paige were on the floor behind the front seat. Call turned the key in the ignition, then slipped the .38 revolver from his boot and placed it next to him on the seat.

"Da-da," Paige said, clapping her hands. "Da-da, Da-da."

"Yes, sweetheart," Haven said. "Hush now. Shh. That's a good girl."

"Da-da," the baby said happily, even louder.

"Your daddy is right there, Paige. See? He's taking us bye-bye."

"You don't have to keep her quiet," Call said, shifting the gears of the station wagon. "Just stay down. This is going to be a bumpy ride, Haven, but at least it won't last long."

He pressed heavily on the gas pedal, and the vehicle surged forward, creating a cloud of thick dust behind it. He whipped around the cabin and onto the rutty dirt road.

Your daddy is right there, Paige, his mind echoed. Damn, what an incredible thing it would be to have a child like Paige.

No, that image was blurring, was slipping out of his reach as quickly as it had come. He had long since accepted that he couldn't have a family: a wife and baby. There was no room, no space, for the thought to settle within his mind. It was too vague—the nameless, faceless child, the unknown woman, his wife. He couldn't grasp it and hold fast as it flitted through his mental vision.

Your daddy is right there, Paige.

Paige. Haven. Haven...Haven...Haven, his brain thundered. *They* didn't skitter away and disappear. They were real, there, staking a claim on... On what? His mind? Yes. And more?

So, okay, he wasn't Paige's father or Haven's husband. But, by damn, neither was Brian Larson. Even if Brian was still alive, he wouldn't deserve to call Haven and that baby his own. Not even close.

Damn it, Shannon, he fumed, pay attention. Only a section of his mind was on full alert for any sign of whoever was following them. He was putting Haven and Paige at risk with his wandering thoughts. *Get it together. Now.*

Call slowed the car as he approached the end of the hopefully hidden road, then pressed on the brake. He leaned forward, scanning the road and land beyond as far as he could see in both directions.

"Call?" Haven said softly.

"It's clear," he said, "but that doesn't mean he's not waiting up ahead past the curve. Stay down, right where you are. If this goes all right, I'll stop on the paved road that leads to my house, and you and Paige can sit where you were before. I don't want anyone on the ranch to know about what happened out here. I've got to think it through first, decide what my next move will be."

"I understand."

Call nodded, then eased the vehicle out from beneath the sheltering canopy of tall trees, and back onto the main dirt road.

Every muscle in his body was tensed to the point of actual pain, his knuckles white from the intensity of his grip on the steering wheel.

He drove at a moderate speed, wishing to arrive at the ranch as quickly as possible, but not wanting to risk losing control of the car if he drove too fast and had to suddenly reach for his gun.

His eyes never stilled, darting back and forth, looking in the mirrors, out the front window, the rear, the sides.

There was no evidence of another vehicle on the road, no telltale dust lingering in the air.

"Okay," Call said, under his breath. "Next time, buddy. Next time, when it's just you and me."

Eight

Call stood with one foot on the bottom board of the wooden fence of the corral. Like the fence that edged the front of his property, all of the corrals were painted pristine white. The large barn beyond was the traditional shade of dark red.

When he'd bought the ranch, everything had been in dire need of paint. He'd hired a crew, had been right in there with them with bucket and brush, and had chosen colors that matched the long-standing image in his mind of what his ranch would look like.

The bunkhouse, as well as the many sheds, was dark brown with white trim. The large, single-story house was brick with white trim. The only thing missing, Call had decided at the time, was a white picket fence around the front yard of the house. That would, in his estimation, give evidence to a woman's whimsical touch. There was no woman; there was no picket fence.

The afternoon was hot, but a cooling breeze saved it from being uncomfortable. The sky was Texas blue—any true Texan believed that it was a less vibrant shade beyond the state's border—and great puffs of white clouds moved slowly across the heavens, making room for the ones behind to follow.

The air was heavy with nature's perfume of wildflowers and the scent of cattle and horses.

The voices of nature intertwined: birds singing, horses whinnying, cattle lowing, a dog barking somewhere in the distance.

And for the first time, Call mused, the delightful sound of a woman's and child's laughter danced through the air on the Triple S.

He folded his arms loosely on the top of the highest slat of the corral, and made no attempt to curb the smile he knew was on his face.

Haven sat on the saddle on the back of a fat, lazy mare that appeared more asleep than awake. Paige was nestled safely in front of Haven on the saddle, and José was slowly, very slowly, leading the horse around the inside edge of the corral.

"Hor-ty," Paige yelled, clapping her hands. "Go, go, go."

Haven laughed. "We're going fast enough, madam. Don't urge this beast to do anything rash."

Call chuckled. "Paige is a natural rider, Haven. She's ready for the big leagues, for speed."

"Not while I'm up here with her," Haven said, laughing. "I don't think she's noticed how far it is from here to the ground."

"Yes, she's ready for a snooze. It's later than usual because she slept in the car, but I think she'll go down now without a fuss."

Call tugged his Stetson roughly forward, shadowing his face.

"José," he said, "help them down. Haven, you take Paige to the room where you and Lupe set up Paige's stuff. I'll meet you in my office."

He turned and strode away, heading for the house.

"Well, fine, sir," Haven said. She glared at Call's retreating broad back, telling herself to ignore that damnable, sexy, loose-hipped walk of his. "At what point in all that do I salute, sir?" She switched her gaze to José. "He certainly got grumpy all of a sudden."

José chuckled, then reached up and took Paige from the saddle.

"Call is a good man, the best," José said. "He just thinks a lot. He keeps many thoughts jarred up inside himself."

"Jarred up?" Haven paused. "Oh, you must mean bottled up."

"*Sí, sí,* that's the one. Bottled up. I can tell he's glad you're here. Call has smiled today. Laughed, too. He doesn't laugh much. No, not much at all. You and your baby, you make him laugh and smile. *Simpático.* Nice, that means 'nice.' He's never brought a woman to this ranch before. *Tu le endulzas su corazón.*"

"Pardon me?"

"Basically that means, 'You warm his heart.'"

Haven glanced once again in the direction Call had gone.

"*Tu le endulzas su corazón,*" she repeated, then sighed. "That's lovely, José, but I'm afraid things aren't always what they seem to be." She forced herself to smile. "Stand back if you value your life. I'm about to attempt to get off this beast."

A half an hour later, Haven stood outside the closed door of Call's office, having asked Lupe where the room was located.

Paige was sleeping soundly in her playpen in one of the guest rooms. Haven had washed her own hands and face, combed her hair, dabbed on some lipstick, then admitted she'd run out of excuses to delay her commanded appearance in Call's office.

She drew a steadying breath, let it out slowly, lifted her chin, then knocked lightly on the door.

"Come in," Call said from within.

Haven entered and closed the door behind her. Her gaze swept over the good-size room, and she immediately liked its welcoming, homey atmosphere.

A large desk was at one end of the room, the top cluttered with papers, folders and magazines. A flagstone fireplace on one wall was banked by floor-to-ceiling bookshelves crammed to overflowing with both hardcover and paperback books.

Two big leather chairs sat in front of the fireplace with a small table between, and a long, oversize leather sofa flanked by end tables and lamps sat against the other wall.

Call stood in front of double glass doors that opened onto a veranda. His hands were shoved into his back pockets, and his Stetson was on the end table next to him.

The bright, summer sun was shining through the sparkling glass doors, backlighting Call, and making it impossible for Haven to discern his expression. He simply appeared massive and powerful. Haven shivered, then wrapped her hands around her elbows.

"Haven," Call said, his voice low, "I appreciate your patience in waiting for the explanation I promised you. Lupe had lunch ready when we got here and ... Well, you've been very tolerant."

"Not really. I was playing ostrich, Call. If we didn't discuss any of this, then I didn't have to deal with it. You're giving me credit that I don't deserve." She sighed. "I guess this can't be postponed any longer."

"No."

Call pulled his hands free of his pockets, and walked to the twin leather chairs by the fireplace. With a sweep of one arm, he indicated that Haven should join him there.

She crossed the room, aware that her legs were trembling, and sank onto one of the butter-soft chairs. Call settled onto the other one.

He immediately leaned forward, rested his elbows on his knees and made a steeple of his long fingers. He stared into the fireplace, a deep frown on his face.

Haven clasped her hands tightly in her lap, her gaze riveted on Call.

The nearly palpable tension was emanating from him again, she realized. It seemed to come in ever-increasing waves that beat against her, increasing her fear of what he was about to say.

Seconds ticked into minutes. The silence in the room was an oppressive weight that made it difficult for Haven to breathe.

"Haven," he finally said, still staring into the fireplace. She jumped as the sudden sound of his voice shattered the silence. "Brian Larson was a traitor to his country. He sold top-secret information to foreign enemy agents.''

Oh, he did not, Haven thought giddily. That was the most absurd thing she'd ever heard. Call was teasing, reciting the plot from a good-guys-and-bad-guys movie he'd seen. How silly, how . . .

She drew a shuddering breath.

Dear heaven, no. The weight of her guilt for what she'd done had been difficult enough to deal with and to find a place for in a dusty, dark corner of her mind.

And now this? Brian a traitor to his own country? If Call was saying it, she knew it was true, but where was she supposed to put it?

She had been Brian's wife, still used his name. What impact was this to have on her life?

Why had that car been following them? Call had made it clear that morning that she was in danger. Why? It was Brian's legacy, Call had said. Oh, it was all too much to handle, just too much.

''Dear God,'' she whispered.

Call shifted to sit back in the chair, then looked directly at her.

''I wish I could soften this somehow,'' he said, still frowning, ''but there's no other way to say it. Brian was a traitor.''

Did she already know all this? he wondered. Was she an accomplished enough actress to have faked the shocked expression, the sudden pallor of her cheeks? No, he just didn't want to believe that.

She was *not* telling him the truth about why she'd married Brian, but her reaction to what he'd just said had been real, honest. His basic instincts as an agent were shouting that message loud and clear. Fine. He'd proceed on that basis.

But, damn it, why wouldn't she trust him enough to confide in him about why she'd married Brian in the first place? He'd told her he wouldn't condemn her for cutting a deal for her brother's freedom.

Didn't she believe him? Believe *in* him? No, she didn't, and that fact was causing a knot to tighten in his gut.

Call pulled himself from his tormenting thoughts. "I don't know exactly when Brian got off the track and chose the wrong road, but I was the one who finally figured out what he was doing."

Haven stared at Call intently as she heard the raw edge to his voice, saw the pain in his dark eyes.

"Oh, Call, I'm sorry," she said, leaning slightly toward him. "It must have been devastating for you to learn that your best friend was a traitor. My heart aches for you."

Confusion showed on Call's face. "You're sorry for *me?* You were married to the man."

"I . . . I hardly knew him," she said quietly, staring at her hands. In the next instant her head snapped up and she looked at Call again. "What I mean is, I didn't know him as well as most women would know a man they agreed to marry. It all happened in a whirlwind, just like a fairy tale. Yes, that's how it was. We went on several dates, then Brian proposed to me, said he wanted me to be his wife, wanted me to have a life far better than the one I had."

"Are you saying you fell in love with him?" Call asked, his voice slightly raspy.

"Well, no, I—Call, I was very young, I was swept off my feet. I suppose I thought I was in love with Brian. I don't know. It seems like it all happened a lifetime ago."

"What about your brother?" he said. *Tell me the truth, Haven.* "What did Brian say about Ted?"

"Nothing, other than he was sorry I'd had a rough time raising my brother."

Call looked up at the ceiling for a moment to rein in his rising temper.

Lies, his mind hammered. Haven was piling up lies like building blocks. If she lied about her marriage, would she lie about knowing that the list existed? Damn it, he'd already decided she *didn't* know Brian was a traitor. The Ping-Pong balls were starting again . . . back and forth, back and forth.

"All right, Haven," he said, a weary quality to his voice. "Brian wined and dined you, made you feel special, and you married him."

"Yes," she said softly.

"He told you he was working on an important project for the government."

"Yes, and that I would be able to help him with it later, but he never said what I would be doing. Call, we were only together for a week or so. Then Brian said he had to go out of town to do some research. Three months went by with no word from him."

She drew a steadying breath, then continued speaking.

"Then the man appeared at my door saying that Brian had died as a result of a hunting accident. I'd hardly had a chance to settle down emotionally when my brother was killed attempting to rob a store.

"By then I knew I was pregnant. After Ted's funeral, I moved to Houston for a fresh start. I was so frightened, so alone, so incredibly young. I didn't live, I existed, one day at a time. But when Paige was born, my whole world changed. She was my source of joy, my reason for being.''

''You have a lot of courage, Haven.''

''Not really. I just did what I had to for myself and my baby. Now you're telling me that Brian was a traitor, and I don't know what that means, I really don't.''

This was it, Call thought, feeling a trickle of sweat run down his back. There was no delaying it, no way to postpone telling her the rest of it.

''Haven,'' he said, his voice gritty, ''there's something else you have to know.'' He got to his feet.

''Yes?'' she said, looking directly at him.

''I was the one... Haven, I shot and killed Brian Larson.''

Call's heart thudded painfully as he saw the color drain from Haven's face. She opened her mouth as though to speak, then shook her head.

An expression of total bewilderment settled onto her pale face, and she cocked her head a little to one side, staring at Call as though he were a stranger she'd never seen before.

She wrapped her hands around her elbows, her back ramrod stiff, as she turned her head to look into the empty hearth.

Call stared up at the ceiling for a long moment, striving for control of his jumbled emotions. He felt completely helpless, his physical strength useless, his analytical mind offering nothing. It was as though he were stripped bare, was vulnerable, had nothing left with which to protect himself.

Haven would now pass sentence on him, condemn him for his actions and label him a killer.

She would draw the circle of sunshine where she and Paige existed tightly around her, and no longer allow him entry into the warm, welcoming space.

He would be flung back into the cold darkness where he belonged. Alone. His jaw was set in a hard line as the silence in the room beat against him with an unrelenting force.

Haven shifted her gaze from the fireplace to Call, looking directly into his eyes.

"If you killed Brian," she said softly, "then he must have been trying to kill *you*. You were defending yourself against an enemy, a traitor, who was determined that no one would stand in his way. It was kill or be killed. Right, Call?"

He frowned, wondering for a confused moment if Haven had actually spoken, or if his frantic mind was taunting him with what he wanted, needed, hoped to hear, yet had not really been said.

"Call? I *am* right, aren't I?"

"Yes," he said, looking at her intently. "Yes, that's exactly how it was."

She nodded. "And you're still torturing yourself with it. You're consumed with guilt because you killed your best friend, a man who had been like a brother to you since you were young boys."

"Yes," he said, his voice rising. "If I had paid closer attention to Brian's actions earlier, I could have stopped him without... That last night wouldn't have happened if I'd been doing what I was trained to do. When I looked back, I could clearly see the clues, the evidence of Brian's betrayal. But it was too late. I'd killed him. I pulled the trigger on that gun and shot him. I quit the agency, walked away. I just couldn't do it anymore. I'm involved now because of you and Paige, and the ugly legacy Brian left behind.''

He drew a shuddering breath, and his voice was raspy with emotion when he spoke again.

''I'm going to protect you and Paige, Haven. I swear to you that no harm will come to you. *This* time, that promise made to a woman and child will be kept. When this is finished, you'll never have to see me again, you won't have to look at the man who killed your husband and the father of your child. But until then, you've got to promise me that you'll do exactly as I tell you.''

Haven got to her feet and lifted her chin. ''No.''

''Damn it,'' he said, dragging one hand through his hair, ''you've got to understand that—''

''No,'' she interrupted, ''it's *your* turn to understand. Listen to me, Call, very carefully. You killed Brian before he could kill you, and I thank God for that. It's time that you destroyed old ghosts. Let it go, Call, and concentrate on now. Do you understand?''

''Haven . . .''

''Do you?''

He stared at her as warring voices hammered in his mind, pulling, pushing, attempting to tear him in two.

He couldn't think clearly, damn it. Haven didn't despise him for killing Brian? She would, once it really sunk in, when she was alone and had to face the truth of what he was and what he'd done.

She'd hate him then.

Wouldn't she?

Or was it possible that she would continue to feel as she did at that moment?

No, no, that was insane.

He was a killer. He . . .

But...

Damn it, he couldn't think!

"Ah, hell," he said.

He gripped her upper arms, pulled her to him and then his mouth swept down to cover hers.

The kiss was tempestuous, searing, evidence of Call's raging emotions. But moments later it gentled as he parted Haven's lips and met her tongue with his own.

He dropped his hands and encircled her with his arms. Of their own volition it seemed, Haven's hands floated upward to wrap around his neck, her fingertips inching into his thick hair. He nestled her to the cradle of his hips, his arousal pressing full and heavy against her.

Desire exploded within Call like a shaft of fire that instantly consumed him. He drank of Haven's sweetness with an urgent thirst, savoring her taste, her aroma of flowers, the feel of her delicate, feminine form molded to his hard, heated body.

He'd experienced rushes of lust before in his life, a driving need to achieve a sexual, physical release as quickly as possible.

But this? It was different, it was more, it was like nothing he'd ever known. Emotions were intertwined with his rising passion. He was registering a fierce protectiveness and possessiveness regarding Haven. No one would hurt her, frighten her, threaten her, because he was there to stand between her and harm's way.

Haven was his!

He lifted his head a fraction of an inch to draw a ragged breath, then captured her mouth once again.

His questing tongue found hers, stroking, dueling, fanning the flames of desire even more.

His mind was far past reasonable, rational thought. If a little voice was clamoring for his attention, demanding that he remember that he came from a dark, cold place, was a world away from Haven's sphere of sunshine and warmth, he didn't hear the message. If he was supposed to remember that Haven was still not being totally honest with him, he didn't care.

All he knew was that Haven was evoking emotions within him that he had never felt toward a woman. All he knew was that his desire had soared to a level nearly beyond his comprehension. All he knew was that he wanted to make love with Haven. *Now.*

"Haven," he said, his voice gritty, "I want you. Oh, how I want you."

Haven heard Call's voice in the distance murmuring her name, telling her of his need to have her. She was surrounded by a hazy, sensual mist. A liquid fire of desire had swept throughout her, causing heat, such incredible heat, and a nameless yearning for something she could not identify. Her breasts were heavy, aching for a soothing touch that she somehow knew Call could bring to her.

She wanted this man, wanted to make love with him, experience the wondrous joining of her body and his. She had engaged in sex with Brian Larson. But with Call? It would be more. They would make love, caring blending with wants and needs. It would be giving and receiving, sharing, creating a memory she would cherish for all time.

"Yes," she whispered, "I want you, too, Call. I want to make love with you."

He framed her face in his hands and kissed her softly, gently, his tongue feathering over her lips and causing her to tremble before he lifted his head again.

Their eyes met, held, mirroring desire at a fever pitch. There was nothing, nor no one, except the two of them, encased in a private, sensuous cocoon.

His smoldering gaze never leaving hers, Call slipped her blouse free of her jeans, then unbuttoned it. He eased it off her shoulders, then released it to fall to the floor. Her lacy bra followed.

Slowly, slowly, he shifted his gaze to her breasts, then lifted his hands to cup the soft bounty in his palms, his thumbs stroking the nipples to taut buttons.

The sensual pleasure of Call's touch caused Haven's breath to catch and the heat of passion to coil tighter deep within her.

She was on fire, going up in flames that licked throughout her. From a distant, passion-laden place, she was vaguely aware of Call unzipping her jeans and slipping them downward, catching her panties with his thumbs as he went. She stepped free of the bulky clothes and the shoes he removed from her feet.

In the next instant he swept her up into his arms and kissed her deeply, causing a purr of pleasure to whisper from her lips.

He crossed the room and laid her gently on the large sofa, his eyes visually tracing every inch of her as he towered above her.

"You're exquisite, Haven," he said, his voice harsh with passion. "Beautiful."

He sat down on the edge of the sofa to tug off his boots and socks, then stood again to shed his clothes.

Haven's heart beat a rapid tattoo as she watched him. The boldness of her scrutiny surprised her, yet in the next instant she realized it felt right, for this was the man she was offering herself to. This magnificent masculine body now being revealed to her would consume her, mesh with her.

The strength that Call possessed could physically crush her, cause her great pain. But she felt no trepidation as he removed his shirt, allowing her to see the actual width of his shoulders and depth of his chest, which was covered in curly black hair.

His arms were perfectly proportioned, the muscles well-defined and developed, she knew, by honest labor, not pumped up at a local health club.

He skimmed his jeans and briefs down his legs, the ropy muscles in his legs again proclaiming the powerfulness of his physique.

Haven's gaze lingered on Call's manhood, his arousal evident, the heightened degree of his need there for her to witness.

He stood perfectly still, giving her time to realize what he would bring to her as a man, granting her the opportunity to refuse this important step with him if she so chose.

She shifted her gaze to meet his eyes once again, then lifted her arms to welcome him into her embrace.

This was Call, her mind hummed, and this was their moment out of time.

He stretched out next to her on the sofa, resting on one forearm, his other hand splayed on her flat stomach.

"You're beautiful, too, Call," she said, looking directly into his dark eyes. "Maybe that's not the proper word to use to describe a man, but I mean it sincerely."

"Thank you." He paused. "Haven, you can still change your mind if you want to. This isn't why I brought you here today, but it *is* about to happen. That is, if you're very sure that this is right for you, that you can promise me you'll have no regrets."

She placed one hand on his cheek. "No regrets, Call. None. I want this every bit as much as you do."

He dipped his head to meet her lips with his as his hand moved slowly lower. After her lips, he sought one breast, drawing the sweet flesh into his mouth.

A gasp of pleasure escaped from Haven's lips. She drew her hands across his shoulders, down his arms, up again to feel the steely muscles in his back, memorizing each tantalizing discovery.

As Call moved to her other breast to pay homage there, his hand covered the nest of curls at the apex of her thighs. She lifted her hips, seeking more, wanting and needing more. Her hands fluttered over him, never still, seemingly everywhere at once.

Call's lips followed the blazing path where his hand had gone, and Haven whimpered, clutching his shoulders with trembling fingers.

"Call, please."

"Soon."

He caressed, stroked, kissed, he, too, discovering the mysteries of who she was, gently, seductively, until a sob caught in her throat. His lips sought hers once more, then he moved over her, then into her.

"Yes. Oh, yes," she said, with a sigh.

They were one.

And it was ecstasy.

He began to move within her, increasing the tempo, feeling her match his raging rhythm, thrusting deeper, then deeper yet. He thundered within her, and she received all that he was.

Call, Haven's mind sang. Never had she experienced anything so wonderful, so perfect. He was lifting her up and away from everything she had ever known. Now her own body was reaching for more, struggling to grasp an unnamed entity that hovered just beyond her reach.

Closer.

She could feel the heated spirals low inside her tightening, coiling into a smaller, more intense circle of sensations.

Closer.

Call's body was her body, hers was his, meshed, one entity. He increased the cadence to a fevered pace, pounding within her, and she rejoiced in the very essence of her femininity that made her the counterpart to this man.

Closer.

And closer yet.

Until...

"Call!"

He felt her reach the summit as the waves rippled through her, drawing him even farther within her. She said his name over and over like a litany, as she dug her fingers into his shoulders. He surged heavily into her one last time to seek his own release, groaning with pure masculine pleasure as his seed spilled from his body into hers.

He collapsed against her, spent, sated, his body glistening with sweat. He buried his face in the crook of her neck, waiting to regain enough strength to move.

"Oh," Haven said, her eyes half-closed, "Call, I never knew how beautiful, how wonderful... Oh, my."

Call chuckled, then moved off of her, resting on his side as he braced his weight on one forearm. He draped his other arm across Haven's waist.

She turned her head to meet his gaze.

"I don't have the words," she said softly, "to describe the beauty of what we shared."

He dipped his head and dropped a quick kiss on her lips.

"You've said it very nicely, Haven. It was special for me, too."

Several minutes passed in a contented, comfortable silence.

In their minds, neither ventured beyond the moment.

They savored now, and it was warm and good.

It was sunshine.

Nine

A short time later, Haven stretched like a lazy kitten, then sighed.

"Well," she said, "back to reality, I guess. We *were* in the middle of a very intense and disturbing discussion."

Call nodded. "There's a washroom through that door in the corner."

Haven looked at him for a long moment, then slid off the sofa, gathered her clothes and crossed the room to enter the bathroom.

Call watched her go, allowing himself the luxury of replaying in his mind the fantastic lovemaking they'd shared. When his body began to respond to the vivid, sensuous scenes in his mental vision, he swore under his breath. He sat up and reached for his clothes.

He'd broken the sacrosanct rule, he mused, as he began to dress. He'd become emotionally involved with the major player in an assignment. So be it. That's how it was.

Later, he'd have to address within himself the issue of his not belonging in Haven's sunshine world. Later.

Now it was back to the business at hand: the danger that Haven was in, the legacy that Brian had left her, the existence of the list, the lies Haven continued to tell him.

"Hell," he said, pulling on his boots.

He stood as Haven reappeared. She started across the room, then stopped in the middle. Before Call even realized he was moving, he had met her there, halfway, opening his arms to welcome her into his embrace.

Haven circled his waist with her arms, and nestled her head against his chest. She could hear the steady thudding of his heart, could feel the tension in his body, the muscles that were tightly coiled.

What the future held for them, she didn't know. All that was important was that very moment, that tick of time where they now existed.

If she was wrong to so quickly dismiss the fact that Call had killed Brian, she didn't care. Brian had been evil, had laid the bricks of the path leading to his death himself, one by one.

She was drawing from inner strengths beyond what she'd known she possessed. She was determined, for reasons not entirely clear to her, to convince Call that Brian's death was not his cross to bear. Call had suffered enough, tortured himself enough, lived with the painful, tormenting memories long enough.

There was something about a woman and child plaguing him, as well. What had happened to them? Who were they?

So many questions.

But first, she knew, they had to address the nightmare that Brian had created.

"Haven," Call said. He kissed the silky curls on the top of her head. "We've got to get to work. There's a major matter of a list of names we need to discuss."

"A list of names?"

"Come sit down, and I'll tell you everything. Did Brian ever mention a list of names?"

She shook her head. "No."

All right, he thought. She either didn't have the list, or didn't *know* she had it. Yes, they certainly did have work to do.

Hours later, Call tapped the pen against the edge of the pad of paper in front of him on the desk. Haven sat in one of the leather chairs that he had pulled across the room to the side of the desk.

He swore under his breath, tossed the pen onto the pad, then leaned back in the chair and glowered at the ceiling.

"Nothing," he said. "We don't know who the man was who came to tell you that Brian had been killed in a hunting accident. Since the agency has only now discovered that you exist, I'm assuming it was an enemy agent who didn't want Solvok's cover blown. Whoever he was, he didn't bring you any of Brian's personal effects. He couldn't, because the agency had them."

"The funeral was a sham," Haven said quietly.

"Yes." He nodded. "I know where and when Brian was buried overseas." He looked at the pad of paper again. "Let's take it from the top. Brian didn't give you an envelope, package—nothing—that he said to keep for him.''

''We've been over this ten times.''

''Then this is the eleventh.''

She threw up her hands in exasperation. ''No, no and no. He didn't give me anything. He said he'd take care of disposing of the household items I owned. Fine. Then he brought home a box full of dishes, bed linens, towels, what have you, that were in no better condition than the ones I'd had. I've slowly replaced those things as I could afford them. He left a few changes of clothes, which I gave to a charity thrift store. That's it . . . end of story.''

''Okay, okay,'' Call said, smiling. He raised both hands in a gesture of peace. ''Don't get your red-headed temper in a rip. You're a tough cookie when you need to be, darlin'.''

She laughed. ''I'm not your darlin','' she said, delivering a now-familiar retort to his use of the endearment.

Call's expression instantly became serious. ''Aren't you?''

Their eyes met, and the embers of desire still within them instantly burst into a raging flame. The remembrance of their lovemaking intertwined with the anticipation of sharing such ecstasy once again, and heartbeats quickened.

Haven finally tore her gaze from his and sighed. ''Call, don't. My mental circuits are on overload. Right now we're having a strictly business discussion. That's all I can handle at one time.''

''Yeah, all right,'' he said, resuming the tapping of the pen against the pad.

"Call, I don't have the list. There's just nothing left from the short time I was with Brian. When I go over in my mind what I've since disposed of, I can't fathom anywhere a list could have been hidden. I realize now that he intended to give it to me because of what he said about me helping him with a project later, but it never happened. He didn't give that list to me, Call."

"You have nothing, absolutely nothing, of a materialistic nature left from the time you were married to Brian?"

"Damn it, Call, no. Would you quit badgering me? Why don't you search my cottage, my car, my—" She stopped speaking, and her eyes widened. "Dear heaven, my car."

Call leaned toward her. "What about it?"

"It was so long ago that I forgot. I don't even know if it's there anymore."

"Your car? That doesn't make sense, Haven."

"No, not my car." She drew a steadying breath. "Calm down, Haven Larson." She nodded. "All right. In the box of household linens that Brian brought to the apartment in Dallas was a lap robe. It was faded and worn, but I rather liked it because it had been handmade, quilted in a rather strange pattern, but it was unique."

"Go on," Call urged, looking at her intently.

"I brought it with me when I moved to Houston. Oh, Call, I'm sorry. It slipped my mind because several months ago I decided it had become so shabby, I'd put it in the trunk of my car along with the flares and first-aid kit." She paused. "I don't know what I'm getting so excited about. It's very thin. It's not a puffy quilt with layers that have been tied through with yarn. There isn't a separate front and back that would enable a list to be hidden in between. Well, dandy. That was a whole flurry of hype for absolutely nothing."

"It's something," he said, "which is more than we had five minutes ago." There was a knock at the office door. "Come in."

Lupe entered with Paige in her arms.

"Mama," the baby said, clapping her hands. "Dada. Mama."

"Oh, so sweet this little one," Lupe said. "She steals hearts with only a smile."

"You must be exhausted, Lupe," Haven said, getting to her feet. "You've been tending to Paige ever since she woke from her nap."

"Oh, no, I'm not tired. This baby makes me float on cloud ten."

"Nine," Call said. "It's cloud nine, Lupe."

"Nine, ten." Lupe shrugged. "It's a lovely cloud no matter its number. I came to tell you both that dinner is ready."

Haven looked at her watch. "I didn't realize it was so late. We have a long drive back into Houston, Call."

"Which you can make after a hot meal," Lupe said firmly. "Wash up now. This baby is hungry. *Sí*, Paige?"

"*Sí, sí, sí,*" Paige repeated merrily.

"What a genius," Haven said, laughing. "My child is bilingual at eighteen months old."

"And beautiful, too, like her mama," Lupe said.

Lupe had that straight, Call thought, getting to his feet. Haven was very beautiful. The lovemaking they'd shared had been beautiful. Kissing, holding, caressing Haven had been . . . Whoa, Shannon. He'd better not dwell on that or his body would betray him and embarrass the hell out of him. It was a proven and humbling fact that his control was slim and none when in close proximity to Haven Larson.

Two hours later, Call drove along the dirt road where he had first seen the telltale cloud of dust revealing the existence of the vehicle following them. He was tense, on full alert, muscles tight, and senses razor-sharp.

A breathtaking, Texas sunset was streaking across the summer sky. As though swept in bold strokes by nature's invisible paintbrush, yellow blended into orange, then magenta, then into deep, rich purple.

Since leaving the agency and starting over at the Triple S, Call had made it a point, for the first time in his life, to stop, take the time to savor the gifts of pure beauty offered to him as the sun rose at dawn, then set again at night.

But at dusk on this night, nature's splendor went unnoticed by Call Shannon. He saw only what might represent danger for Haven and Paige.

As his eyes flickered back and forth between the rearview and side mirrors, his mind was pulled back into the world of darkness and evil, where he had existed for so many years. There was no beauty, no innocence, within his sweeping view.

He glanced at Haven and saw how tightly she was clasping her hands in her lap. She hadn't spoken since they'd left the ranch. Paige's nonsensical chatter that was directed at Susie, the bedraggled cloth doll, was the only sound in the car.

Lord, he thought, redirecting his attention to the road, he didn't want to take Haven back into Houston. He wanted to keep her at the ranch with him where she would be safe, protected, out of harm's way.

His suggestion to Haven after dinner that she stay overnight at the ranch had been flatly refused. She was not, she assured him, breaking her promise to follow orders. She simply wasn't prepared, as she'd packed only enough needed supplies for Paige to last the day.

There was also, she reminded him, the fact that Call wanted to retrieve the worn, faded quilt from the trunk of her car.

Her arguments for returning to Houston that night were sound, Call silently admitted. The agent part of him knew that to draw out into the open whoever was dogging them, Haven must go about business as usual.

But the section of him that was a man besieged by foreign emotions he'd never experienced before, had wanted to bar the door and refuse to allow her to leave the ranch house.

He wanted her close to him so he could protect her.

He wanted her close to him so he could make love with her.

He wanted her close to him because Haven was his.

Call shook his head in self-disgust as he realized he was once again not addressing the issue of his past in regard to a future with Haven.

She had seemed to accept, to his total amazement, the fact that he had been the one who had killed Brian. But how would she feel once she'd had time to be alone and square off against the truth?

Forget it, Shannon, he admonished himself. His full attention now should be, and would be, directed toward ensuring the safety of Haven and Paige.

"Haven," he said, glancing over at her, "I'm going to turn off up ahead here to get gas in the car.

There's a station in the middle of nowhere that all the ranchers in this area use. There's a good old boy that runs it. I think he's been there since the beginning of time.''

Haven smiled. ''It's nice to know that there's something left from another era.''

''There you go,'' he said, as he drove onto another dirt road. ''Hank is definitely from another era.''

''Will the station be open this late?''

''He never really closes it. He lives in a trailer next to it, and will fill your tank in the middle of the night if need be. He figures that if you want gas at 2:00 a.m., then he'll give you gas at 2:00 a.m.''

Haven laughed softly, then looked back to check on Paige. The baby was still jabbering to her cloth doll.

The gas station, Haven instantly decided when she saw it, was so awful, it was wonderful.

There was one ancient pump nearly devoid of paint and displaying a great deal of rust. A metal post that stood about ten feet tall and curved at the top, held a yellow light bulb that cast a dingy glow over the area. A multitude of bugs danced in front of the bulb in the gathering dusk.

Old tires, car parts and a slew of undefinable junk were heaped next to a small wooden building that looked as though it could be carried off by a strong wind. In the dirty window of the building, a bright pink neon sign reading Goat blinked on and off.

''Goat?'' Haven said.

Call chuckled. ''There was, according to Hank, a bar named The Golden Goat in this area that got plowed under when the freeway crossed through. Someone took off with the *The* and *Golden* parts of the sign. Hank got the *Goat*. He says it adds class to the place.''

''I love it,'' Haven said laughing.

And he, Call thought, as he turned off the ignition, better watch his step or he was liable to end up falling in love with Haven. He *did not* fit in in Haven's sunshine world, and he'd save himself a lot of heartache if he'd remember that.

He beeped the horn, then opened the car door.

''You and Paige stay put,'' he said, glancing over at Haven. She nodded. ''This won't take too long.''

On the far side of the wooden building was a round-topped, silver trailer that displayed rusted and dented evidence of age. The door was flung open, and a short, wiry man emerged, snapping suspenders into place as he clopped down the three rickety steps to the ground.

He had white hair that appeared to have only a nodding acquaintance with a comb. His skin was wrinkled and leathery from years spent in the blazing Texas sun. A stubble of white beard covered the lower half of his face, and the suspenders that he'd tended to held up faded, baggy trousers topped by a dingy gray undershirt.

''Hell's fire, Call,'' Hank said, ''can't a man eat his supper in peace?''

''Nope,'' Call said. He inwardly groaned, knowing that the ritual of Hank's complaints would have to be completed before one drop of gas left the ancient pump.

Hank squinted as he peered through the front window of the car. ''Well, now, lookee here. That's one pretty little gal you've got there, Call.'' He paused and leaned forward. "Is that ... I'll be hog-tied, sure enough. That there's a baby."

"Really?" Call said, raising his eyebrows. "Hell, I didn't know there was a kid in my car. How about some gas, Hank?"

"Keep your britches on, boy. You've already caused my supper to go stone-cold, so don't make it worse by trying to get me to move at big-city speed. Then again, if I pump you some gas you'll leave me in peace."

"There you go."

Hank lifted the nozzle from the bracket, cranked a handle several times, then proceeded with the process of filling Call's gas tank.

"Speaking of the big city," Call said casually, "did you happen to see a vehicle today that doesn't belong in these parts?"

Hank rubbed one hand over the bristle on his chin, then shook his head.

"Nope," he said, "can't say as I saw any strangers. Not today, or any other that I can recall."

"I just wondered."

"You're sure puttin' the miles on this piece of junk you're drivin' here. I just filled this tank a couple days ago, and you're already ridin' on near empty."

Call frowned. "You gassed up the station wagon?"

"Yeah. José was drivin'. He was actin' like he had bitin' ants in his britches, real jumpylike, and tellin' me to hurry on up 'cause he had things to do. I set him straight right quick. Ole' Hank doesn't move any faster than I decide I'm goin' to."

"Did José mention where he was headed?"

"Nope. Hell, Call, he's your foreman. Seems to me you oughta know what errand you sent him on. If José is drivin' a Triple S vehicle, it stands to reason that he's tendin' to Triple S business."

"Yeah, he was. Just slipped my mind, is all."

"You were probably wool-gathering about that pretty little gal sittin' there in the car." Hank cackled. "So, who is she?"

"I'm not saying. You're a worse gossip than a bunch of women talking over the back fence. I'm just going to keep quiet, and let you worry about it."

"Hell's fire."

A few minutes later, Call drove away from the gas station, honking the horn once as a message of goodbye. He was soon back on the main dirt road.

José, he mused, had left the ranch in the station wagon without Call realizing it, and had driven a distance great enough to use a lot of gas.

Where had José been going? Why hadn't he told Call that he was leaving the ranch? There was also the incident that morning of José acting strangely, refusing to look Call straight in the eye when they were talking. He'd dismissed the incident as an overreaction on his part, but now... Damn it, what was José doing that he didn't want Call to know about?

Call narrowed his eyes and his grip on the steering wheel tightened.

He didn't like this, not one damn bit. José's strange and secretive behavior was taking place at the exact same time as the discovery of Haven's existence and Call's involvement in the assignment centered on her.

"Damn," he said.

"What's wrong?" Haven said.

"Nothing. I was thinking about something, that's all. Haven, I'm going to be watching your place through the night. I'll be outside, unseen, but you can sleep easy because I *will* be there. Tomorrow I'll put the wheels in motion to have you guarded twenty-four hours a day until this thing is settled.''

Haven sighed. ''I don't like the sound of that. I'll feel as though I'm in a goldfish bowl.''

Call smiled over at her. ''Yes, well, you'll be a safe goldfish, darlin'.''

Haven laughed softly in spite of herself, then allowed the word *darlin'* to tiptoe around her heart.

Night nudged the last, lingering streaks of the colorful sunset into oblivion. As darkness fell with a heavy curtain, stars began to blink on, glittering like diamonds in the obsidian sky.

Haven told herself to blank her mind and savor the beauty of the night, the close proximity of Call and the knowledge that her baby, having given up the battle against sleep, was safe and only an arm's reach away.

But as each mile covered brought them nearer to Houston, reality gained force and replaced her tranquil thoughts with harsh ones.

It seemed impossible, she realized, that it had been only the regulation number of hours of one day since Call had arrived at her cottage to pick her and Paige up to go to the Triple S.

So much had happened during that time span that it was nearly beyond comprehension.

The nightmare, the haunting, tormenting memories of the past that centered on Brian had been brought to the fore, forcing her to relive them. Even more, Brian's evil legacy was placing her and Paige in harm's way now. It was as though Brian was reaching out from the grave to snare them, fling them into an arena of danger.

Haven shivered, then turned her head to look out the side window of the car.

She needed to separate herself from Call for the remainder of the drive, take time to sift and sort through so many complicated and confusing issues.

Call Shannon had shot and killed Brian Larson.

Haven moved the stark fact through her mind, heart, her very soul. She took a deep breath for courage, then waited for the verdict from her inner being as to how she must now truly and honestly view Call.

She mustn't soften, nor cloud, the truth of what Call had done.

What Call had done, her mind echoed over and over.

Yes, he had killed Brian, but if he hadn't pulled the trigger on that gun, it would be Call who was buried in a faraway country.

Call had not killed his lifelong friend, because that man had no longer existed as Call had known and loved him. The person who had died had been a traitor to his country, an adversary, who had been fully prepared to kill Call if need be.

She had long since distanced herself from Brian Larson. He had been her husband and Paige's father, but those facts didn't matter in the day-to-day course of life. Nor was it important in the present scheme of things that it had been Call Shannon who had ended Brian's life.

Call was Call as she knew him now.

What Call had done.

Sensual images of the lovemaking shared with him flitted in her mental vision in tantalizing, vivid detail. He had awakened her femininity, evoked desire within her for the first time in her life. He had shown her the wondrous, glorious meaning of making love instead of just engaging in sex.

It had been ecstasy, splendor beyond description, and the remembrance of it caused a flush to stain her cheeks and a pulsing heat to thrum low within her.

What Call had done.

She looked over at him, seeing the strength and power of his body, savoring his aroma of fresh air, soap and man, remembering the salty taste when she'd flicked her tongue over his tanned skin.

He had irrevocably changed her life, was staking a claim on her heart that was frightening and exciting in the same breathless moment.

Was she falling in love with Call Shannon? she wondered. She didn't know, nor did she have the emotional energy at this point to pursue the question. All she could do was deal with events as they unfolded in regard to her feelings for Call, and the dark danger caused by Brian's past action.

"Haven," Call said, bringing her from her tangled thoughts, "we'll be at your place in a few minutes. I'll carry Paige in, you get her diaper bag. I'll come back out for the playpen."

"All right."

"I'm going to get the quilt from the trunk of your car and drape it over the playpen as though you've decided to store it in your bungalow that way. If you're being watched, and I assume you are, we'll have to hope your shadow doesn't know a lot about babies, won't realize you need the playpen set up for Paige, not stored away. It's not great, but it's the best plan I can come up with."

Haven drew a wobbly breath. "Okay."

"Hey," he said gently, glancing over at her quickly, "hang in there. You're doing fine, just fine."

"I think I'm under control, but then a wave of fear washes over me, and I feel as though I'm crumbling."

"That's understandable. Just remember what I said. Nothing is going to happen to you and Paige. *Nothing.*"

Haven nodded, and they drove the remaining distance to her cottage in silence, each lost in their own thoughts.

Call parked the station wagon next to Haven's car, and they proceeded with the plan he'd outlined. Paige opened her eyes as he lifted out the car seat, frowned up at him and began to whine and wiggle, obviously none-too-pleased at having her sleep disturbed.

"You'll be in your own bed in a few minutes," Call said to the baby, as they walked along the sidewalk. "Mellow out, little lady."

"No, no, no," Paige said.

"Whatever," he said absently.

His eyes darted back and forth, his senses on full alert for any sign of trouble. Someone was out there—he knew it—and burning fury born of frustration churned within him.

As they approached Haven's door, she took her key from her purse.

"Put the diaper bag down," Call said, when they stopped. "Give me the key and take Paige. I want to go inside ahead of you."

Haven did as instructed, Call entered the living room, and turned on a light. Haven was right behind them, carrying a fussing Paige.

"Damn it to hell," Call said.

Haven's eyes widened in horror and the air seemed to swish from her lungs, making it nearly impossible to breathe. Her heart beat with a wild and painful cadence.

The room had been trashed.

Books were strewn everywhere, the sofa cushions had been sliced open and the foam yanked free. The drawers of the end tables were on the floor, the contents dumped out. Pictures from the walls had been broken, the glass and frames shattered.

"Dear God," Haven whispered, as tears filled her eyes. "No."

Ten

The light from the lamps in the living room of the hotel suite cast a soft glow over the bedroom beyond.

Call stood next to the bed where Haven slept, his dark brows knitted in a frown. He lifted one hand with the urge to place it gently on Haven's pale cheek, but seconds later dropped his hand back to his side.

He drew a deep breath, then let it out slowly, striving once again to maintain control of the raging anger that churned like molten lava within him.

His gaze skittered to the crib where Paige was sleeping peacefully, her bottom poked up in the air, her thumb in her mouth.

As he looked at Haven again, his jaw tightened even more as the events of several hours before pounded against his brain.

Haven's entire cottage had been thoroughly searched with no regard for the damage being done.

Even the fluffy pillows he had somehow known would decorate her bed had been cut open and the stuffing pulled free. Paige's room, the bathroom and kitchen were all a disaster—ransacked, destroyed. Nothing had been spared.

Brian's legacy, Call thought bitterly. Since Solvok had surfaced, the foreign enemy agents had obviously learned of the possibility of Haven having the list. They'd come, searched, and there was no way to know at that point what they might have found.

Haven had moved like someone in a semitrance, not speaking, as she surveyed the destruction of her home. She had been...still was...deathly pale, and had not seemed to comprehend what Call had been saying to her.

He had made the necessary telephone calls, which resulted in three unmarked, dark cars arriving at the cottage, spilling out a total of six agents in various modes of dress.

The flurry of activity had brought Marian Smith, Haven's neighbor, baby-sitter and friend, bustling over to the cottage in obvious concern. With one of the agents in tow, Call had sent Haven and Paige to Marian's bungalow. Whether the older woman wondered why no city police cars had been on the scene, he didn't know.

Call had barked orders at the agents, telling them there was no point in dusting for fingerprints as the people they were dealing with would not have made the mistake of leaving any. They were to put Haven's home back together as much as was possible, while making a detailed list of what had been destroyed beyond repair.

When Call reached for the telephone again, he'd punched in a number he would probably never be able to forget, but had never used before that night. The clicking sounds he had heard told him that the call was being scrambled, sent through an untraceable series of power stations to reach its destination and finally produce the voice Call wanted to hear.

"MacIntosh."

"Shannon," Call had said, his voice raspy with his rising fury. "I want to see you, face-to-face, tonight. Don't even think about arguing with me, MacIntosh. Just listen up and do it."

A weary sigh escaped from Call's lips as he continued to stare at Haven.

She didn't deserve to go through this crap, he inwardly fumed. Frightened, confused, physically and emotionally exhausted, she had evoked so many emotions within him, they had tumbled together in a maze, making it impossible to discern one from the next.

The only thing that was crystal clear, was that he wanted to carry her away from the ugliness, this dark side of life, and take her to a sunshine place where he could protect her and her baby, that beautiful, innocent baby.

But he couldn't do that, he knew it, and the realization of that fact was coiling painfully in his gut.

A soft knock at the door to the living room caused him to snap his head around. He looked once more at Haven, then left the bedroom, pulling the door to within an inch of closing. He strode across the large, plushly furnished main room.

"Yeah," he said, standing to one side of the door.

"Room service."

"Coffee?"

"Two pots of coffee, very hot, exactly like you ordered."

The prearranged code had been properly executed,
but Call still drew the gun from inside his boot, clicked
off the safety, then inched forward enough to peer
through the small, round hole in the door. Satisfied,
he slipped the chain free, opened the door and stepped
back.

A cart containing two silver pots of coffee and several covered dishes was pushed quickly into the room
by a man wearing white trousers and a royal blue
smock. Call relocked the door.

"MacIntosh," Call said, nodding slightly at the
man.

Peter MacIntosh took off the smock to reveal his
traditional white suit. He looked pointedly at the gun
in Call's hand.

"Yeah, all right," Call said. He flipped the safety
catch into place and slid the gun back into his boot.

"Well, boy," Peter said, folding his arms over his
chest, "you've got gall, I'll say that for you. I can't
think of another agent who would phone me, give me
orders and expect me to carry them out."

"You're here, aren't you?" he said, glaring at Peter.

"I am," he said, nodding. He settled into an easy
chair. "From what I heard in your voice on the phone,
I was afraid you'd take a couple of my men apart just
because they happened to be there."

"Could have happened." Call ran one hand over the
back of his neck, then sank into the easy chair facing
Peter. "Hell, what a mess."

"It came down fast, that's for damn sure. You were
just barely ahead of the foreign elements in getting

Haven Larson.'' Peter paused, placing his elbows on the arms of the chair and tented his fingers. "You said on the telephone that Haven is innocent of any wrongdoing, that she was Brian's victim, his pawn. You reached that conclusion very quickly, Call. I assume she confirmed our theory of having married Larson in exchange for her brother's freedom?''

Call narrowed his eyes. "Don't push me, Mac-Intosh. Haven's innocence isn't up for debate, or a vote. It's a fact, pure and simple.''

Peter looked at him for a long, intense moment, then finally nodded. "Bring me up-to-date on what has transpired. You do realize, of course, that the less-than-savory are no doubt perfectly aware of Haven's present whereabouts.''

"I know that. I'm also assuming they were watching every move we made when we arrived at Haven's. They'll have picked up on the fact that no city police were called to the scene, and they're now prepared to go up against government agents.''

Peter nodded.

"I want Haven and Paige here because I can protect them. This hotel is literally crawling with agents that I put into place.''

"You ruffled some upstairs feathers with that maneuver,'' Peter said, chuckling.

"Tough. The suits in their ivory tower pushed my buttons to get me to agree to take on this assignment. If they don't like the way I'm carrying it out, that's their problem. I don't want to hear about it.''

"Fair enough.''

Call leaned forward, braced his elbows on his knees and laced his fingers.

"Okay, MacIntosh, this is what I've got so far.''

Call related the events of the day. Peter listened without commenting, or interrupting to ask questions. His expression was bland, revealing no emotion. It would appear to a stranger observing the interchange that Peter MacIntosh was bordering on bored, but was too polite to express that fact.

But Call knew Peter, knew that the dapper little man was committing to memory every word spoken, and as he listened a portion of his brain was already weighing and measuring the possible options of action to be taken.

"I have the quilt from the trunk of Haven's car," Call said finally. "I haven't had time to examine it as I was getting Haven and Paige settled in here. I packed up some of their things from the cottage, collected them from Marian Smith's bungalow and left the agents I called in to straighten Haven's place as best they could. Haven isn't functioning to a great degree. She's shell-shocked, vague, operating in a type of trance."

"You've seen that reaction before."

"Yes, I have, but I wish Brian was still alive so I could tear him limb from limb for doing this to her." Call laughed, a short, harsh, bitter-sounding noise. "That's great. I killed him once. Now I'd like nothing better than to have the opportunity to do it again."

"I don't find that surprising or shocking under the circumstances, Call." Peter tapped his fingertips together as he stared up at the ceiling, a frown now on his face. He looked at Call again. "Do you want an in-depth check run on José?"

Call swore under his breath, and leaned back in the chair.

"I want to say no," he said, "but I can't. José's unusual behavior is setting off alarms in my brain that can't be ignored. Damn it, Lupe and José are like family to me. They're..." He stopped speaking, and a shadow of pain flickered in his eyes. "Hell, what difference does *that* make? Brian Larson and I were as close as brothers for countless years, and look what that got me. Run a thorough check on José. Was a check run on Marian Smith?"

"Yes, as well as Haven's other neighbors, but you know that phony data can be put into place by powerful countries. Call, what's your plan? Tomorrow is Sunday, but I imagine that Haven is due at work Monday morning."

"She is. We chatted about that today at the Triple S. I wondered how she could raise a child on what I assumed was minimum wage made as a clerk in a store.

"It turns out that she is practically managing the place. The woman who owns it is getting up in years, and has trained Haven in a broad spectrum of areas. The owner works there on the weekends, that's it. I want a check run on the owner of the boutique, too.

"Haven places all the orders for new merchandise, and the owner no longer asks to see the order forms before they're sent. Haven isn't making big bucks, by any means, but her salary and responsibilities are more than I thought they were. She would definitely *not* take kindly to my saying she was to stay put here come Monday morning."

"The dust won't have settled on this situation by then, Call."

"Yes, I know. I've got to give more thought to that situation, so I can spell it out for Haven as to exactly what she is to do."

"No, Call. Enough is enough."

At the sound of Haven's voice, Call lunged to his feet to face her. Peter eased himself upward in an inbred gesture of rising when a woman enters the room.

Haven crossed the room to stand in front of Call. She wore a long, pink cotton nightgown that Call had snatched off the hook on the back of the bathroom door in her cottage. Since he hadn't thought to pack her robe, she'd draped one of Paige's crib blankets around her shoulders like a shawl. Both of her hands gripped the soft material tightly in front of her.

"Hello, Mrs. Larson," Peter said. "Please allow me to introduce myself. I'm Peter Smith."

"No, sir, you are not," she said, looking directly at him. "Your name is MacIntosh. Whether or not your first name is actually Peter is of little significance to me. What is important is that I have overheard a great deal of the conversation taking place in this room." She switched her gaze to Call and lifted her chin. "I repeat, enough is enough. Sit down, gentlemen, because I fully intend to have my say."

"Now, Haven..." Call started, raising both hands.

She narrowed her eyes. "Sit down."

Call sat.

Peter camouflaged a threatening burst of laughter by coughing as he settled back into his chair. His total attention was directed at Haven. He once again adopted an expression of bland observation, but even with his strong control over what he chose to reveal on his face, nothing could hide the merriment dancing in his eyes.

"Thank you," Haven said stiffly. "Please do not interrupt while I am speaking."

One of Call's hands splayed on his stomach of its own volition it seemed, as he had the sudden sensation of having been punched in the gut. He stared intently at Haven, and his mouth dropped slightly open.

He loved her, he thought incredulously. He was in love with Haven Larson.

A trickle of sweat ran down his back.

There she stood, looking like a disheveled urchin, her silky curls in wild disarray from sleep, and her once-pale cheeks flushed by the intensity of her determination to be heard.

The nightgown she wore had the simplicity of youth and innocence, and her baby-blanket shawl was endearingly absurd. The toes that peeked from beneath the hem of the gown revealed toenails polished with a soft shade of pink.

If a stranger entered the room at that moment and swept a cursory glance over Haven, he might conclude that she was a vulnerable child.

But Haven Larson was most definitely a woman, Call thought. She stood ready to take on both himself and Peter; she was prepared to slay the dragons.

She was magnificent.

She was his.

And, heaven help him, he loved her with every breath in his body.

"Call," Haven said, "close your mouth. You look like a goldfish."

Call snapped his mouth closed.

Peter smothered a chuckle with another coughing fit.

Haven cleared her throat and squared her shoulders.

"Now, then," she said, "I realize that my reaction to what had been done to my home was not a performance that I can be proud of."

"It was perfectly normal to—" Call began.

"Mr. Shannon," she said, "I have the floor."

"Sorry," he mumbled, and sank a tad lower in the chair.

"The initial shock has worn off. I am now just rip-roaring angry. Evil hands have touched my personal possessions and those of my child, all because Brian Larson walked in, then out, of my life."

She took a deep breath, then continued speaking.

"Call, I realize that I said I would follow your orders to the letter during this nightmare. However, I can no longer do that. I won't be wrapped in cotton and tucked away in a safe corner until this situation is brought to a proper end.

"Those people, those enemy agents, have gone too far. I have the right to defend what is mine. I heard you say, Call, that you had yet to decide what directives to give me regarding my going to work Monday.

"Well, from this moment forward I will have a voice in decisions of that nature. The change in my position in this matter is not open for discussion or debate. It is an etched-in-stone fact."

"Bravo," Peter said, smiling. He raised his eyebrows as he looked at Call. "Well? I do believe, my boy, that the ball is in your court."

Call shot Peter a dark glare, then planted his hands on the arms of the chair. He got slowly, very slowly, to his feet.

As Haven watched him rise, she was unable to gauge his state of mind as there was no readable expression on his face. His measured ascent made him appear overwhelmingly tall, powerful and incredibly male.

She forced herself not to move, not to take a step backward. The sudden wobbly condition of her legs would have to be ignored, while maintaining a lingering hope that they would support her long enough to stand her ground.

Call looked at Haven for a seemingly endless moment, and she met and held his gaze, determined not to be the first to look away. Silence hung heavily in the air.

"Haven," Call said. His voice seemed unnaturally loud as it shattered the stillness. Haven jerked, but didn't retreat. "Would you care to sit down?" he continued, sweeping one arm in the direction of the chair he'd just vacated.

"Yes, I believe I would," she said. She stepped forward and sank into the chair, stifling the grateful sigh that threatened to escape from her lips. "Thank you."

She crossed her legs, then smoothed out her nightgown with one hand, the other still firmly clutching her baby-blanket shawl.

"That was an interesting dissertation you just delivered," Call said. There was a rather matter-of-fact tone to his voice. A bevy of butterflies swished into Haven's stomach. "Yes, very interesting." He paused, strolled three feet in one direction, reversed his trek, then stopped at the spot where he'd originally stood. "I have no problem with your altered stand on this issue."

Haven's eyes widened. "You don't?"

"You don't?" Peter echoed, frowning.

"No, not at all," Call said pleasantly. "Your opinions, input, suggestions, will all be weighed and measured for merit. If you wish to go to work Monday, then you'll go to work Monday. If you want to return to your cottage tomorrow, instead of staying here at the hotel, that's perfectly fine, too."

Peter narrowed his eyes as he stared at Call as though attempting to peer into the younger man's brain.

He could not, Peter decided, remember when he'd enjoyed something as much as he was the scenario unfolding before him. Call had an ace to play, no doubt about it. He was biding his time, picking his moment, and Peter wouldn't miss this for the world.

Call Shannon, Peter mused on, had also met his match in the form of the enchanting Haven Larson. Big, strong, tough Call was going down for the count at the hands of a delicate and delightful woman. Cupid had scored a direct hit on this lonely and taciturn man, whom he loved like a son. He could only hope that Call would not withdraw into his dark, cold world, and lose the warmth and wondrous beauty within his reach.

"Peter is going to take the quilt with him," Call rambled on, "and have it examined by the powers that be." He glanced at Peter. "The quilt is over there on the sofa, MacIntosh." He looked at Haven again. "The next move in any plan of action can't be completely formulated until we know if that quilt is a significant part of this package. Do note the word *we*, darlin'. Yes, indeed, you'll be consulted every inch of the way."

"What's the catch, Mr. Shannon?" Haven said, eyeing him warily.

Call took one step forward, planted his hands on the arms of Haven's chair and leaned toward her to speak a minute distance from her lips. His eyes were locked with hers, and a pulse began to beat wildly in his temple.

"The catch, Ms. Larson," he said, his voice low and tense, "is that whether you decide to go to work, return to your apartment or hide in a broom closet, I'm going to be so close to you every damn minute that when you inhale, I'll exhale.

"I would have stayed in the shadows to watch over you, not invaded your space twenty-four hours a day, but you cooked that with your sassy little speech. We're doing this *my* way, and that's the end of that story."

"But..."

"Haven," he said, shifting his hands to her upper arms. He hauled her to her feet. "Just shut the hell up."

Then his mouth melted over hers.

That, Peter MacIntosh thought, getting to his feet, was quite an ace.

He crossed the room, picked up the quilt, then went to the door. With one hand on the doorknob, he turned to see Haven's arms float up to encircle Call's neck, causing her baby-blanket shawl to fall unheeded to the floor. Call dropped his hands from her arms to gather her close as the kiss went on and on.

Peter smiled and nodded in satisfaction, then left the suite, closing the door behind him with a quiet click.

Eleven

In a minute, crystal-clear section of Call's mind, he registered the information that Peter had collected the quilt, left the room, and the lock had snapped into place. The agents Call had ordered into action were on duty; no one could get through that door to the suite.

The remainder of his mind was encased in a hazy, sensual mist centered on Haven. He drew a quick, rough breath, then captured her mouth again, his tongue delving into the sweet darkness to find hers.

Emotions slammed against his mind, then his heart, and his very soul. He was holding, kissing, wanting with an intensity that was deeper than any he'd ever known, the woman who had stolen his heart for all time, the woman he loved.

The sensual promise of what he would share with Haven when he meshed his body with hers was creating a flame of passion that raged unchecked throughout him. He felt her tremble in his arms, and heard a soft whimper escape from her lips.

Lord, how he loved this woman.

Haven tightened her arms around Call's neck to give her the strength to stand. Heat invaded her body, consuming her, causing a sweet ache low within her. She was acutely aware of every inch of her own body, and once again rejoiced in her femininity that Call had awakened from a lifelong sleep.

The depth of her need, of her desire for Call didn't frighten, nor embarrass her, because it was right, and good and meant to be. She would give of herself totally, and be filled with immeasurable joy as Call returned that giving in kind.

Call Shannon, her heart whispered. Dear heaven, was she falling in love with this man? Was love part of the tangled maze of emotions in her mind? She didn't know, and at that moment she couldn't think. She could only want, and burn with the need of him.

But no, wait, her mind urged. She had to talk to Call, had to tell him . . .

She shifted her hands to his chest and pushed gently, breaking the kiss. Call looked at her questioningly as she eased out of his arms, wrapping her hands around her elbows.

"Haven, what . . ." he started, his voice rough with passion.

"There's something I have to talk to you about, Call." She drew a trembling breath, then met his gaze. "I heard you tell Mr. MacIntosh that I was innocent of any wrongdoing. Then he asked you if I had told you why I married Brian."

"Haven..."

"Call, please, just listen, hear me out. It meant so much to me to hear you defending me, making it clear that you trusted me. Trust is such a precious gift, and it's time that I returned it in kind. I realize that there's every chance you'll think poorly of me when I tell you the truth, but that's a risk I have to run.

"Call, I *did* make a deal with Brian Larson. I married him in exchange for my brother's freedom. There were no social dates of courting. There was no fairy-tale romance. It was cold and clinical...a business transaction."

"You don't have to do this, Haven. Let it alone."

She shook her head. "No. I want you to know that *I* trust *you*. That's so important. Even if you condemn me for what I did, despite your saying earlier that you wouldn't, I'll know I was completely honest with you."

Call nodded, a frown on his face.

"I didn't love Brian," she said, her voice quivering. "I didn't even like him. We agreed on a bargain, a shabby trade. I'd tried so hard to raise my brother properly, but he was wild, reckless, so angry at the world. I couldn't control Ted. He wouldn't listen to me."

"That wasn't your fault."

"I don't know if it was or wasn't. I was so young. Ted was arrested...again...and I knew he was guilty, would go to prison. There was nothing I could do to stop it from happening. Brian appeared out of nowhere, just arrived at my front door."

"And made his offer."

"Yes. If I married him, he'd see to it that Ted went free."

"Haven, what did Brian say to you? What explanation did he give for wanting you to marry him?"

"He said he worked for the government, and he was up for a promotion. The position he was being considered for called for a very stable, down-to-earth man. He figured if he was married, he'd stand a much better chance of being chosen for the job. He also said that there would be a special project I would be able to help him with but, as you know, I never knew what it was."

"Smooth, very smooth."

"Oh, he was charming, never stopped smiling when he presented his plan. I was emotionally drained, and terribly frightened for Ted." She paused, then shook her head. "No, there's no excuse for what I did. I agreed to Brian's proposition. I submitted to him when he demanded that our marriage be consummated."

Damn it to hell, Call thought. Fury slammed against his mind, causing a knot to tighten with an angry fist in his gut. He hated the idea of Brian touching Haven, using her body for his own pleasure and physical release. Had he hurt her? Taken her roughly like he would a common woman from the street?

"I see your disgust and anger now," Haven went on, a sob catching in her throat, "and I deserve it. I sold myself to Brian, just like a hooker standing on the street corner." Two tears slid down her cheeks. "But, Call? You have to know this.... If I had it to do over again, I would do the exact same thing. From that horrible nightmare came my baby, my precious Paige. My life began, really began, on the day she was born.

Can you understand that? I love my baby so very much."

Call looked at Haven for a long moment; then his expression gentled, the anger gone.

"Thank you," he said quietly.

"Pardon me?" She dashed the tears from her cheeks.

"Thank you for trusting me. You told me it was time for me to put my ghosts about Brian to rest. Well, you need to do that, too. I don't condemn you for what you did. I swear I don't. I understand, Haven." He opened his arms to her. "Come here."

She literally flew into his embrace, and he held her fast. She tilted her head back and spoke close to his lips.

"Make love to me, Call. Please?"

He swept her up into his arms, kissed her deeply, then strode across the room to the second bedroom on the opposite side of the living room.

The lamps from the main room cast a rosy glow over the bed. He set her on her feet, then framed her face in his hands.

"Haven," he said, "I . . ." *I love you. Oh, Haven, I love you so damn much.*

The words hammered in his mind, but he couldn't speak them aloud. A dark, cold fist clutched his soul with a sudden force that caused a shudder to rip through him. He couldn't declare his love for her, had no right to stake a claim on her—or the warm sunshine of her world. He could only *make* love with her, and somehow, *somehow,* convince himself that that was enough.

Now, at this moment, Haven was his. He couldn't, wouldn't, think beyond this point in time.

"Call?" Haven said. Her voice quivered as she searched his face for the meaning of his long silence and intense scrutiny. "Is something wrong?"

His answer came in the form of a searing kiss that took her breath away. It was a hungry kiss—urgent, delivering a message that she was unable to comprehend.

Liquid fire coursed throughout her, pushing aside her momentary confusion, allowing passion to reign supreme. She met his tongue boldly with her own, stroking, teasing, dueling, until a groan rumbled in Call's throat.

They stepped apart only long enough to shed their clothes with shaking hands, then reached eagerly for each other once again. They tumbled onto the bed, not stopping to throw back the blankets.

Hands and lips roamed, caressed, explored and discovered anew, all that they were, all they would give, all they would receive.

Sensuous currents wove throughout them, around them, heightening their senses even more, making every touch, taste, aroma, sharp and vital, and causing desire to reach a fever pitch.

"Call. Please."

He thrust deep within her in one smooth, powerful motion, filling her. His control was gone, had been flung beyond his reach as the moist darkness of her femininity received him, tightened around him in a welcoming embrace.

He thundered within her in an ever-increasing tempo that she matched beat for beat. She wrapped her legs around him and lifted her hips, urging him on, deeper, harder, wanting more, and more, and more.

It was rough, near-violent, tempestuous.

Wondrous.

It was ecstasy.

Only a racing heartbeat apart, they burst upon the place they sought, holding fast to each other, calling the name of the other, not wishing to end their exquisitely beautiful journey.

They lingered there, high above forever, sated, savoring, memorizing, then slowly, serenely, drifted back to now.

Call rolled to his side, drawing Haven close to him. Their breathing gentled, and all was quiet. Neither moved, nor spoke, not wanting to shatter the sensuous spell that was still a nearly palpable entity surrounding them.

Just before Haven gave way to the somnolence claiming her, a niggling little voice in the far recesses of her mind questioned the existence of the ghost that remained, haunting Call.

Who were the woman and child he'd made veiled references to? What had happened to them? What secret still stood as a barrier between her and Call?

Several hours later, Call stirred and opened his eyes. Years of conditioning caused him to become instantly alert with no lingering fogginess of sleep.

He lay perfectly still, listening for the slightest sound that might have brought him from his deep, peaceful sleep. He heard nothing, nor did his instincts detect any hint that anything was wrong.

Haven was curled against him in an unconscious attempt to seek the heat from his body. He gazed at her, marveling again at her delicate beauty.

Memories of their lovemaking washed over him, and his body tightened as the embers of desire still within him began to flare once more into licking flames.

He edged carefully off the bed, not wishing to disturb her, and managed to draw back the blankets, slipping her beneath their warmth. She moved restlessly in her sleep for a moment, then settled again with a soft sigh.

"Call," she murmured.

A strange achiness gripped his throat as he stood next to the bed, drinking in the sight of her.

She was dreaming of him, had spoken his name from the depths of her slumber. Why that fact was so special, had touched him so deeply, he couldn't fathom. It was, he supposed, another facet of this thing called love, being in love, making love, none of which he had ever experienced before. Never before Haven.

Call turned and left the bedroom with the intention of making certain that all was as it should be in the suite. When he checked on Paige, he did not even attempt to hide his smile as he gazed down at the peacefully sleeping baby. He snapped off the lamps in the living room, and hesitated only for a moment as his eyes quickly adjusted to the sudden darkness.

After easing back onto the bed, he gently straightened the blankets across Haven's shoulders, then settled onto his pillow, one arm beneath his head.

His mind skittered to the remembrance of Haven's feisty performance of her sermonette declaring her new and active role in the dangerous scenario they were involved in.

His counterattack of telling her to go for it, do what she wanted to, with the proviso that he would be as close to her as her own shadow, had not been a great move on his part. It was going to be much more difficult to protect Haven the way things now stood.

Call sighed, then frowned as he stared up at the ceiling.

Well, one thing was a given, he thought dryly. He didn't behave true to form when it came to interacting with Haven Larson.

But never before Haven had he loved.

He pulled his mind from where he was focused totally on Haven, and spread out in his mental vision all the facts he'd gathered regarding the situation created by Brian. His frown deepened even more as he again acknowledged that José was high on the list of people to be investigated as possible enemy agents.

Lord, he didn't want José to be anything other than the loyal, trustworthy friend he'd been since Call had met him. Yet, there was no ignoring the fact that José was involved in something that he did not want Call to be aware of.

And if José was guilty, where did that leave Lupe? They were deeply in love, devoted to each other. It just didn't work in the agent-oriented part of his reasoning that Lupe wouldn't know what José was doing.

"Damn," Call said aloud.

He glanced quickly at Haven to see if his outburst had disturbed her. She slept blissfully on.

For the next several hours, Call sifted and sorted through the data in his brain, realizing no concrete plan of action could be formulated until Peter Mac-Intosh reported back about the quilt.

That quilt was a long shot, he mused. He'd only had a cursory glance at the faded and worn blanket, but it had been enough of a scrutiny to make him believe that it wasn't remotely connected to the missing list.

Over and over again, Call reviewed the details of what he knew, weighing and measuring, hoping to discover something that had slipped by him. No new revelation presented itself, and he finally gave in to the fatigue that tugged at him, and slept.

Haven stood in her living room, her eyes sweeping over all within her view. Call was next to her holding Paige, who was chattering away while patting Call's nose.

"Well," Haven started, then stopped. She drew a steadying breath and lifted her chin. "Your men did a wonderful job of setting things to rights. I certainly do appreciate their efforts on my behalf."

She walked to the front of the sofa and stared at the black electrician's tape zigzagged across the cushions where they had been sliced.

"Yes, I certainly do appreciate—my goodness, the walls are sooty. You can see the outline of where the pictures were hung. A person just isn't aware of how grimy things have become until they remove what was previously there. That's interesting, don't you think? Yes, it is, because . . ."

"Haven," Call said gently.

"No," she said sharply, wrapping her hands around her elbows. "Don't say anything kind, or nice," she said, her voice trembling. "Just don't, Call. I'm going to be strong through this. I have to be to maintain my self-respect, to be the woman I've become since Paige was born. I can't lean on you, Call, use your strength instead of reaching deep within myself for my own. Can you understand that?"

Ah, Haven, Call thought. He loved her so damn much. That love was growing, as incredible as that seemed, with each new layer of herself that she revealed to him.

He wanted to holler the roof down, tell her that he loved her, and because of that love, she could lean on him as much as she needed to.

He would protect her.

He would have enough strength for both of them.

He would see this mess through to its proper end.

But he couldn't, wouldn't, do any of that. A small section of the complicated and confusing emotion of love was, at that moment, moving free of the tangled maze. It was slowly changing from a fuzzy, unclear entity to one that was in sharp relief, providing him, with crystal clarity, the knowledge of what he should do. He sure as hell didn't like what he'd just discovered, but that fact couldn't come into play.

He must love Haven enough to step back, grant her the freedom to accomplish what she desired to do in this dangerous situation, in a manner that would meet *her* needs, not his. Her personal integrity, her sense of self—both were on the line here. He respected that, could relate to that. So be it.

"I understand, Haven," he said quietly.

She frowned slightly, a rather puzzled expression on her face. He held her gaze as she studied him. She nodded, then dropped her arms to her sides as she realized her self-protective gesture was no longer necessary.

"Thank you, Call," she whispered. "Thank you very much."

And along with the heartfelt thanks given to Call, she now knew, went her love. In the midst of all the chaos, the bizarre and frightening events she'd been swept up into because of Brian's treachery, the franticness and chilling fear, there was a small circle of warm sunshine that was steadily growing larger.

Within that sphere, that space to be cherished, she could see herself in her mental vision, the sunlight flowing over her in a glorious cascade. She was smiling gently, a womanly smile, serene in the knowledge that she loved.

At the edge of the circle, still in the shadows beyond, was Call. She opened her arms to welcome him into her embrace, to come forward to bask in the warmth of the sunshine and of her love.

But in the vivid scenario unfolding so clearly in her mind's eye, Call didn't move. He didn't take the steps needed to join her. That symbolism that represented the returning of her love in kind, didn't take place.

A shiver coursed through Haven, and cold fingers touched her heart, her soul. She felt alone, and lonely, and incredibly sad.

"Haven," Call said, jarring her from her thoughts. He set Paige on her feet, and the baby toddled across the room, holding Susie, the cloth doll, by one foot. "Once this thing is settled, and I can get the proper people working on it, you'll be compensated for the damage done to your possessions."

She glanced around, her eyes lingering an extra moment on the stiff, black tape crisscrossing the sofa.

"Oh," she said, meeting his gaze again, "that never occurred to me. I mean, it's not the government's fault that I married Brian. This—" she swept one arm in the air "—is my price to pay for a decision *I* made."

"No, it's not," he said, his jaw tightening slightly. "You'll also receive the money that is due you as Brian's widow."

Haven shook her head. "No, Call, I couldn't accept that money. Funds to replace the furniture and other things that were destroyed here...yes, all right, because this is Paige's home, too, and I don't want her reminded on a daily basis of the violence that took place. But the other money? No, I don't want it."

"It's legally yours."

"Morally it's not."

Call opened his mouth to retort, then snapped it closed again as he realized that a flash of hot anger had surfaced within him. He stared up at the ceiling for a long moment, then let out a pent-up breath as he strove to rein in his temper.

He raised one hand in a gesture of peace, then shifted his gaze to Haven, his eyes instantly widening as he saw the expression on her face.

"Darlin'," he said, unable to contain a burst of laughter, "you look like an explosion ready to happen."

"Don't you laugh at me, Call Shannon," she said, squinting at him.

"I wouldn't dream of it," he said, still grinning. "Even an old cowboy like me knows when to fold his cards." His smile faded. "The issue of Brian's benefits can go on the back burner for now. You have enough on your plate to deal with."

"You're right," she said, with a sigh.

"There you go. If you'd keep in mind that I'm right more than I'm wrong, you could save yourself a lot of fussing."

"Oh, good night," she said, rolling her eyes heavenward, "here comes another dose of cocky and arrogant."

And she even loved that exasperating part of him.

And the way he said "darlin'" in a voice so darn sexy, it caused shivers to slither down her spine.

And his habit of slipping in "There you go," wherever it fit.

And that walk of his? Heavenly days, that walk.

And his compelling dark eyes, and the wondrous ecstasy that took place when he took her into his arms and...

Oh, Haven, Haven, Haven, she admonished herself, why not just face facts as they stood? She loved Call Shannon.

For the first time in her life she was in love—totally, absolutely, irrevocably. That Call did not return that love in kind was a given. She was walking right smack-dab toward a future that would cause her heart to break and her tears to flow, but there was no way to stop the journey.

Because she loved him.

"Well, I've got to get going," Call said.

He took off his Stetson, raked one hand through his hair, then settled the hat back into place, tugging it low on his forehead, shadowing his features.

Darn and damn, Haven thought, her gaze riveted on him. The take-off-your-Stetson-so-you-can-put-it-back-on malarkey was Texas personified. She'd seen it done countless times over the years by the cowboys who were the real goods.

And, oh, heavenly days, was Call Shannon ever the real goods.

The gesture-by-rote with the Stetson took on a whole new meaning when executed by Call. It was blatant masculinity, earthy, rugged and so incredibly male, it made her weak in the knees.

She would not, Haven told herself firmly, dash across the room and start tearing the clothes from Call's magnificent body. That was a delicious thought, but definitely not ladylike.

A funny little noise, which Haven had to admit was an adolescent-sounding giggle, escaped from her lips, and a flush of embarrassment stained her cheeks.

"Do you have a problem?" Call said, frowning.

"Problem? Me? Oh, no, not at all." She waved one hand breezily in the air.

"Right," he said, eyeing her warily.

Paige wandered over to Haven and wrapped her tiny arms around one of Haven's knees.

"Mama," the baby said. "Up."

Haven lifted her and settled her onto one hip.

"You're ready for lunch, then a nap," Haven said, then kissed Paige on the forehead.

"I'll be back as soon as I can, Haven," Call said. "I've got to cover some things with MacIntosh." Such as the check he'd had run on José and others, what had—if anything—been discovered about the quilt, the word from intelligence sources as to how far spread was the fact that Haven existed and was connected to the list. "Don't go outside, or open the door to anyone you don't know. There's an agent out there watching over you, so there's nothing to worry about. I'll—"

He stopped speaking as a knock sounded at the door.

"Stay put," he said.

"Roll over," Haven said, wrinkling her nose at him. "Fetch the newspaper."

Call shot her a dark glare, then went to one of the windows.

"Marian Smith," he said. He moved to the door, unlocked and opened it. "Hi, Marian."

"Hello, hello, Call," she said, bustling into the room. "Hello, Haven, and my sweet Paige. I've brought you lunch in my trusty picnic hamper. Isn't this fun?"

She glanced around. "Well, this is an improvement over how things looked last night. I hope the police catch those nasty hoodlums who upset you so terribly, Haven. It was sinful, that's what it was.

"But this is a new day, and we'll put all that behind us. We'll have a picnic right here at your kitchen table. I feel the heat so, you know, dear. It's much too warm for me in the courtyard."

"An inside picnic is just fine," Call said. "I'll leave you to enjoy yourselves."

"Won't you join us, Call?" Marian said.

"No, ma'am, I have an appointment."

He crossed the room, slid his hand to the back of Haven's neck and dropped a quick kiss on her lips.

"Lock up behind me, Haven," he said.

He ruffled Paige's hair, touched the brim of his hat with one fingertip when he looked at Marian, then left the cottage.

"Oh, Haven," Marian said, beaming, "I do declare that he is the sexiest thing in a pair of jeans that I've seen in all my born days."

"Good grief," Haven said, laughing, "let's have some lunch."

Call tossed the papers onto Peter MacIntosh's desk, then walked slowly to the gleaming windows. He narrowed his eyes as he stared at the skyline of Houston, then turned to look at Peter. The older man sat in the chair behind the huge desk, his attire, as usual, totally white.

"I'll be damned," Call said. "So that's what José was so jumpy about."

Peter nodded. "No one has approached him, Call. I didn't want to take any action on it until I'd talked to you."

"José smuggled his seventeen-year-old nephew into this country from Mexico," Call said, shaking his head. "Are your sources certain that Lupe knows nothing about this?"

"Yes. José didn't want Lupe involved in case it went bad. José's nephew inadvertently walked into a drug transaction in progress, and those folks don't like witnesses. The kid's life was in danger. José put together a plan, and you have company in the hayloft of your barn. José has no idea that we know."

"Leave it like that."

"Come on, Call, I can't . . ."

"Leave it, Pete," he said, his voice low. There was a steely edge to the words spoken, a nearly palpable element that Peter had encountered before in dealings with Call Shannon. "The agency has looked the other way on a helluva lot of things when it suited their needs. This is small pickings, not worth the paperwork to document it. A seventeen-year-old kid's life is hanging, Pete. Leave it. Alone."

Peter looked at Call for a long moment. It was eye-to-eye, man to man, and neither flinched. A stranger might view the exchange as two adversaries squared off, ready to draw blood if need be. What wasn't visible was the high regard, respect and caring, each man had for the other.

Finally Peter nodded slowly. "This one is yours, Call. I never heard of José's nephew."

"There you go," Call said quietly.

Call's gratitude had been expressed. Peter understood and accepted it. The subject was closed.

"So," Peter said, "the issue at hand. Everyone you wanted checks run on is clean. Word in the trenches is that Haven's existence in regard to Brian is not widely known as yet. However, Solvok's people knew early on. What they were waiting for was Solvok to resurface to determine if he had the list. To cover their butts, Haven has been watched since Solvok went underground."

Call stiffened, every muscle in his body tensing. "What?"

"You heard it. They knew about her, but we didn't. They want that list, Call. They would have preferred to obtain it as planned, but they'll settle for this as second best. We'd be forced to pull all those agents out of active duty, not just move them around. There's a lot of names. We'd be caught short in some very hot spots, and you can be damned sure they'd take advantage of that situation."

"Damn."

"In spades. However, that's not how it's going down because *we* have the list. The quilt."

"That faded old blanket had the list sewn into it?" Call said.

"No, not exactly. Sewn *onto* it, is closer to the mark. The top stitching that creates a pattern was irregular, unusual. Indeed it was. It was a code, a stitched-in-thread code, of the agents' names. Our boys cracked it a few hours ago. Things are moving very quickly overseas, and our people will be taken care of. We'll put the word out as soon as it's safe for our agents that Haven has nothing of value that once belonged to Brian Larson."

"But for the next handful of hours, she's still in danger."

"Yes."

Call picked up the papers again from Peter's desk.

"No one here is a threat to her," he said, "but someone out there is. Someone who has been around awhile, and is in a position to keep close tabs on her. Who in the hell—" He stopped, the sudden tight coiling knot in his gut causing him to hiss in his breath from the pain. "God, where is my brain? How could I have been so stupid?"

"Call?"

"This is my fault. I promised to protect Haven and Paige. I swore I would, and I delivered them right into the hands of—it's just like before, Pete. The other time...dead...the mother, the baby...the innocent...Dear God, what have I done?"

He turned and started toward the door.

"Call, wait," Peter said, lunging to his feet. "Who is it? Who is the threat to Haven and her baby?"

Call yanked open the door, then hesitated only a moment to look back over one shoulder at Peter. Call's eyes held a mixed message of fury and pain.

"Marian Smith," he said, his voice a hoarse whisper.

Twelve

Haven took a deep breath, then let it out slowly while she closed her eyes, struggling for control. She felt as though a scream were caught in her throat, threatening to break free—a scream, born of her terror, that would go on, and on, and on.

If she gave way to the near-paralyzing fear consuming her, she knew she would be useless, totally at the mercy of the evil people who now held her and Paige captive.

She opened her eyes, and once again scrutinized the room. It was approximately twenty feet square. A small window high on one wall allowed a minuscule amount of sunlight to cut through the gloom, but the rays did not take the edge off the damp chill.

Marian Smith sat on a straight wooden chair at the far side of the expanse, humming softly as she knitted. She pulled the yarn from the tote bag. That same bag had contained the gun that had materialized the moment that the picnic lunch had been eaten.

Haven sat on a cot next to the wall. Paige was sleeping peacefully on her tummy, one blanket beneath her and another covering her.

The only sounds in the dreary room was the maddening click of Marian's knitting needles, and her off-key humming of a song Haven didn't recognize.

Haven squared her shoulders, and stared directly at the older woman.

"Marian . . ."

"I've told you not to speak," she said. Her voice had a pleasant, casual, chit-chatty tone to it. She continued to knit, not looking at Haven. "You really must do as I say, dear."

"I have the right to know what you plan to do with me and my baby. Dear God, Marian, you've taken care of Paige for so many months, watched her grow, saw her first steps, heard her first words. Don't you have any feelings for her at all?"

"Of course I do," she said, still concentrating on her knitting. "She's a darling child, but my mission comes first, always has. I'll be very relieved to leave that shabby bungalow where I've been forced to live. I'm accustomed to far better. This assignment is nearly over, and it's none too soon for me."

"What do you want from me, Marian? Why are you doing this?"

Marian stopped working on the craft, and looked at Haven.

"Come now, Haven, let's not play games. The question of whether or not you have the list Brian

Larson was to deliver was answered the moment that Call Shannon showed up. We know who he is, and his sudden appearance told us what we needed to know. He is, admittedly, a formidable opponent, but we can deal with him.''

"I don't have any list," she said, her voice rising.

"Don't shout, or I'll have to insist that you not speak at all. Granted, there are only cartons of kitchen appliances in this warehouse so no one will hear you, but your yelling would get on my nerves.''

"What are you going to do with me and my baby?'' Haven said, forcing herself to speak quietly.

"My goodness, dear, that's not up to me.''

"Then who—''

"It's very simple," Marian interrupted. She began knitting again. "My colleague, Gerald, whom you will be meeting soon, is now making the necessary telephone call to deliver the message that will determine your fate.''

"What message?''

"Your lover, your oh-so-handsome Call Shannon, either turns over the list to us, or you and Paige will die.''

Call stood in Haven's living room, staring at Paige's cloth doll, Susie, which he clutched tightly in one hand.

"I'm sorry, Call," the man next to him said. "I saw you let Marian Smith in here, so I figured she was clean. When Haven and the baby left with Marian, I assumed you knew about it.''

Call turned to the man, who was in his early thirties, was about six feet tall and powerfully built. He had blond, sun-streaked hair that was badly in need of a trim, a deep tan and blue eyes. In jeans and a faded, green T-shirt, he looked like a man who would prefer to be surfing off the coast of California.

But, Call knew, Tux Bishop was a top-notch agent, one of the best. Not only were his physical skills extraordinary, but he also had nurtured to a high level an inherited seed of psychic powers that he tapped into by deep meditation.

"It's my fault, Tux," Call said. He looked at the cloth doll again. "Damn it, I screwed this up so badly, it's a sin. I promised Haven that I'd protect her, would see to it that no harm came to her or Paige. They're innocent victims...." He stopped speaking and shook his head as his emotions choked off his words.

Tux frowned as he studied Call, seeing the fury and pain in Call's eyes, hearing it in his voice.

"If anything happens to them, I'll..."

"Whoa." A smile broke across Tux's face, making him appear even younger. "We're the Dynamic Duo when we work together. Flash and Dash. We'll be hearing pretty quickly, I imagine, from the creeps that have Haven and Paige. Then, buddy, you and I are going to go in and get your lady and your kid. No doubt about it."

Before Call could reply, the telephone rang, causing both men's heads to snap around to stare at the source of the shrill sound. Call snatched up the receiver.

"Call Shannon."

"Good day to you, Mr. Shannon," a deep voice said. "I trust that you're well?"

"Cut the bull," he said, a muscle jumping along his jaw. "What's the setup?"

Call listened, his grips on the receiver and the cloth doll tightening to the point of making his knuckles turn white.

"Understood," he said finally, "but you understand this. If anything happens to Haven Larson or her baby, there won't be anywhere for you to go that I can't find you. You'll be a dead man."

Call slammed down the receiver, and turned to Tux.

"They want the list," Call said. "They're holding Haven and Paige in warehouse eight on Warehouse Row. I'm to take the list there—alone—and exchange it for Haven and the baby."

"When?"

"Midnight."

"Excellent. Let's get the blueprints of the building, and map out a plan."

"Tux..."

"Let's move, Call. We've got a date to rendezvous with a couple of snazzy blondes. By the way, you're squeezing the stuffing out of that doll."

Call looked at the toy, surprised to find it still in his hand. He lightened his grip on it.

"This is Paige's favorite doll. Haven made it for her, and Paige doesn't like to be without it for long. I'm going to get Haven and Paige out of there, Tux. Whatever it takes, I'm going to bring them home."

Just before twelve o'clock that night, Call and Tux stood at the rear of warehouse seven, their gazes sweeping over building eight, which was fifty feet away.

"Set?" Call said.

"Yep."

"Go."

As Tux disappeared into the darkness, Call shrugged into a lightweight Windbreaker to conceal his shoulder holster, which held a 9 mm Beretta semi-automatic pistol.

He glanced at his watch, then remained where he was, waiting for the prearranged time to elapse to allow Tux to get into place. He centered his attention on warehouse eight again, narrowing his eyes.

Haven was in there, his mind taunted. Haven and Paige were depending on him to come get them, lead them safely out, take them home.

His life was in that building.

He dragged both hands down his face, then drew a deep breath, letting it out slowly.

It was necessary, he knew, to reach deep within himself to grasp the abilities he'd fine-tuned as an agent. He had to put aside the raging emotions that were focused on Haven and Paige, blank his mind to make it possible to perform at maximum.

He closed his eyes, turning mentally inward, became acutely aware of every muscle in his body. His senses heightened, accentuating sounds and smells. He could feel the prickly sensation of the hair on his arms, heard the echo of his own steady heartbeat.

Nodding in satisfaction, he opened his eyes, looked at his watch, then started toward warehouse eight.

Haven stood in the doorway to the small room with Marian to her right and just inches behind her. Paige slept soundly on the cot, oblivious to the dangerous drama unfolding around her.

The main area of the warehouse was dimly lit by banks of fluorescent lights suspended from the ceiling by chains. The multitude of large boxes were stacked in varying heights, appearing like evil sentries.

Gerald stood in the gloomy glow of one of the banks of lights. He was facing the door, which was about one hundred feet away at the far side of the building.

Haven shivered as she looked at Gerald. Her reaction to him when she'd met him hours before had been the same: chilling fear and heartfelt loathing.

That man, she knew, was fully prepared to kill her and Paige, and at that moment stood ready and waiting for Call's arrival.

Another man was out there, too, hidden in the shadows. She'd had a brief glimpse of him when Marian had instructed her to move to the doorway. Call would see Gerald, but wouldn't know of the other man's existence, wouldn't realize that another was set to ambush him.

She felt torn in two, a part of her mentally begging Call to hurry, to end this horror, to lead her and Paige out of harm's way.

But another section of her being willed the door that Gerald watched not to open, not to reveal Call, who would be stepping into an arena of danger and possible death.

She wanted to scream aloud to Call, tell him to run as fast and as far as he could.

And she wanted him to appear in all his magnificent splendor, big and strong, sure and powerful, and carry her and Paige from the darkness into the sunshine.

"Midnight," Marian said, bringing Haven from her tormented reverie. "Your lover is due any second now, Haven. Remember your instructions. You're to stand perfectly still, here in the doorway where he can clearly see you." She took the gun from the tote bag and pointed it at Haven waist-high. "And clearly see this. Don't speak. Not one whisper of sound is to come from you. Understand?"

Haven nodded, her gaze riveted on the door across the expanse of the warehouse. Her breath caught as the door opened and Call stood silhouetted in the doorway, backlit by the millions of stars in the heavens.

"Good evening, Mr. Shannon," Gerald said. "Do come in and join us. Close the door, please, and then raise your hands."

Call did as instructed as his eyes darted quickly around, weighing and measuring all that he saw. He forced himself not to linger on Haven, not to answer the directives of his heart that would spin his quieted emotions out of control.

"Do you have the list?" Gerald said.

"I have it," Call said.

"Come closer, please, easy and slow—no sudden moves." Gerald raised one hand to point a gun directly at Call. "Do note that Marian is holding a weapon that is directed at Haven. Your lady's life and that of her child are in your hands."

Sudden blinding and chilling memories slammed against Call's brain with painful intensity, memories of a horror long past of another woman and child he had promised to protect. A woman and child who had died because he had not done what he'd sworn to do.

He shook his head slightly, and with every ounce of willpower and mental command he possessed, forced the hated memories back into the far recesses of his mind. He moved slowly forward, inching his way carefully to the right, instead of following a straight course to Gerald.

"That will do," Gerald said, when Call was fifteen feet from him. "Stop there."

Bingo, Call thought. Perfect. Any second now he should hear a three-beat tapping of a gun against metal, telling him that Tux was in place and ready. This plan had to be executed without the slightest flaw, because Marian Smith was holding a gun on Haven, and wouldn't hesitate to pull the trigger.

"The list, Mr. Shannon?" Gerald said.

"Come on, Gerald," Call said, with a snort of disgust. "You're not dealing with a rookie here. I want Haven and Paige out here, standing halfway between you and me."

"Ah, the mighty agent barks his orders," Gerald said. "You seem to be forgetting that you're at a distinct disadvantage. The weapons are in *our* hands. You have no defense."

Wrong, Call thought, as he heard the three-beat pinging sound he'd been waiting for.

Bedlam erupted in a blur of motion and noise.

Call lowered his body and lunged farther to the right, straightening immediately again as he set one shoulder against the bottom box of a tall tower. The weight of his fully propelled and tense body caused the huge boxes to topple forward.

"No!" Gerald yelled.

At the same instant that the boxes crashed down upon Gerald, a metal air vent was kicked free and Tux dropped into sight to the floor, landing lightly on the balls of his feet.

"Surprise," he said, as he pointed a gun at the man hiding in the shadows. "Drop the piece and hit the deck. Dead or alive...your choice."

The man dropped the gun, and sprawled onto the floor, spread-eagle on his stomach.

Haven gasped as the two high-speed scenarios took place before her within seconds. The explosion of violence and sound jolted her into action of her own. She knocked the gun from Marian's hand, sending it skittering across the floor and out of reach.

In the next instant, Haven made a fist of her right hand, pulled back her arm and delivered a solid blow to Marian's jaw. Haven watched in fascination as Marian crumbled into a silent lump on the floor.

Call ran across the warehouse and grasped Haven by the upper arms, searching her face.

"Are you all right?" he said. "God, Haven, please, tell me that you and Paige are all right."

"Yes. Yes, Call," she said. Unexpected tears filled her eyes as she smiled at him. "We're both fine."

"Mama," Paige whined, from the cot.

"I'll get her," Call said. He went to the cot and lifted Paige, holding her tightly to his chest. "You're okay, baby," he murmured. "Nothing happened to you. You're alive, and you're okay."

Haven frowned slightly in confusion and concern at the sound of the raw emotion evident in Call's voice.

"Howdy, ma'am," Tux said to Haven, as he came to the room. "Tux Bishop at your service. I just dropped in."

"Thank you so much," she said. "I knew that other man was there, but I couldn't warn Call. I should have realized he'd be prepared for something like that. I'm so glad this nightmare is over."

"Call," Tux said, "I cuffed the three scums to a metal support post. Do you know that was a refrigerator you dumped on your buddy Gerald? That boy is going to be a walking bruise. Hey, that's my blond gal you're holding there. Give me that kid. I like babies. They're soft, they smell good and they don't argue about soup to nuts like the all-grown-up variety." He crossed the room and took Paige from Call's arms. "Whoa. Aren't you a pretty picture? You're going to break hearts later on, sugar babe."

"She slept through the whole thing," Haven said.

"Well, sure," Tux said. "She's made of tough stuff. You've got a mean right cross there, yourself, Haven. I sure wouldn't want you mad at me."

"Da-da," Paige said, patting Tux's cheek.

"I'm putty in her hands," Tux said. "Let's go to my car and call in for some backup to pick up these nasty folks. Okay, Paige?"

" 'Kay, 'kay, 'kay," Paige said merrily.

"Back in a few," Tux said, leaving the room with Paige.

In the suddenly quiet room, Haven stared at Call, and he met her gaze, no readable expression on his face. She wanted to run into his arms, savor his aroma, feel the wondrous strength in his arms as he held her fast.

But she didn't move. There was something wrong, an invisible something, that seemed to be standing between her and Call as solidly as a brick wall.

"Call?" she said, unable to keep her voice from trembling.

"I'm sorry, Haven," he said, his voice low and flat. "I promised to keep you safe and I failed. I swore that nothing would happen to you or Paige and—"

"You couldn't have known that Marian Smith was part of this."

"Damn it," he yelled, "I should have had her checked out further, dug deeper. There's no room for mistakes in this type of thing because it means people will die, and too many people have died because of me. Too damn many! I let you down, Haven, and you know it."

"No, Call, you came for us. We're all right."

"It should never have come to this," he said, his voice flat again. "It's my fault."

"Call, don't."

"I have no choice, because it's true. I love you, Haven, and I nearly got you killed."

"What? You . . . you love me?"

"Yeah. Yeah, I love you," he said, a bitter edge to his voice. "That must thrill the socks off you. The man who loves you couldn't even keep you safe from harm."

Haven took one step toward him, but stopped as she again felt the nearly tangible wall, the high barrier Call had erected between them.

"The Triple S," he said. "You asked me once who the other two Ss were for. They were Shannons . . . my sister and her year-old son. Cathy was young, innocent, got mixed-up with a bad crowd. She was sixteen, got pregnant and came to me for help. Our folks couldn't handle it. They were older—been gone a couple of years now."

He drew in a shuddering breath.

"I set Cathy up in an apartment where she would be safe. I made certain she took proper care of herself during the pregnancy. When I was away on assignments, I made arrangements for her to be looked after. She had a boy, David Call Shannon.

"I was involved in a messy assignment that spilled into this country instead of being entirely overseas as my assignments generally are. I wanted to send Cathy and David Call away until I could get things squared away, but she wouldn't go."

He stared up at the ceiling for a long moment, striving for control of his emotions. He looked at Haven again, and fresh tears filled her eyes as she saw the anguish on his face.

"I told Cathy I'd protect her from harm. I promised her that she and David Call would be safe. One night we were going to the grocery store. The phone rang, and I gave her the car keys and told her I'd be right there. She apparently decided to warm up the car and...the car...exploded. It was a bomb meant for me. Cathy and David Call were killed."

"Oh, dear God, Call," Haven said, two tears spilling onto her cheeks. "I'm sorry. I'm so very sorry."

"That was six years ago. And now, it's history repeating itself. I promised to protect you and Paige. I failed. Go back to your sunshine world. I'll stay in my dark one. The more distance you put between yourself and me, the safer you'll be."

"No. No, you can't dismiss me just like that. I love you, Call Shannon."

"Then you're a fool, Haven Larson."

"Hey, Call," Tux yelled from the larger part of the warehouse, "backup is here for our friends."

"Goodbye, Haven," Call said, then strode from the room.

"Wait," she whispered. "Dear heaven, Call, wait." She hurried out of the room.

Call went to where Tux stood holding Paige. Four men in suits and ties came through the main door of the warehouse.

"This is one great kid you've got here, Call," Tux said, jiggling a gurgling Paige in his arms.

"Take them home, Tux," Call said, a steely edge to his voice. "Let the suits finish up here. I want you to take Haven and Paige home where they belong."

Frowning in confusion, Tux watched Call stride toward the outer door. Tux turned to look at Haven where she stood ten feet back.

She was ramrod stiff, her chin lifted, shoulders squared, as her gaze followed Call out of the warehouse.

But silent tears of heartache streamed down her face.

Thirteen

Call tested the fence post for steadiness, nodded in satisfaction, then slid a glance toward José and Gilbert, José's nephew.

Gilbert was coming along just fine, Call mused. He was eager to please and eager to learn, and José was extremely patient as he taught the boy the skills needed on a working ranch.

MacIntosh had come through with the necessary documents to allow Gilbert to stay at the Triple S with a green card identifying Call as his sponsor. The boy would have a chance now; he had his future spread before him, waiting for choices to be made as to which road to travel.

Call sighed and looked off into the distance, not seeing the brilliant blue sky or the lazy cattle grazing. The image in his mental vision was Haven.

During the two weeks since he'd left Haven and Paige in Tux's safekeeping in the warehouse, Haven had never been far from Call's thoughts.

He missed her, ached for her and, oh, Lord, how he loved her.

Her image in his mind's eye was so vivid, so real, that he felt at times she was actually there, within his reach.

But that wasn't true, and when the realization slammed against his heart and mind, he was consumed by a chilling loneliness that touched his very soul.

He'd done the right thing when he'd walked out of Haven's life. His world of darkness did not mesh with hers of sunshine.

His lack of foresight regarding Marian Smith had nearly cost Haven and Paige their lives. Just as with Cathy and David Call, the evil tentacles of his dark world had crept into a place where they didn't belong, and innocents were put in harm's way.

To ensure Haven's safety, he had to stay far away from her. Forever. But, damn, it hurt. It was a searing pain within him that he could only hope time would quell.

The sound of an approaching horse brought Call from his tormented thoughts, and he was grateful for the diversion. He looked up at the ranch hand who reined in his horse.

"What's doing, Jack?" Call said. "You're in a hurry about something."

"Lupe sent me," Jack said. "She said a special delivery came for you, and you'd best get back to the house."

Call frowned. "What was delivered?"

"Beats me," Jack said, with a shrug. "Lupe just said to come get you because you had to tend to it right away. She said split-lickety, which I figured meant lickety-split, so I hightailed it out here."

"There you go," Call said, tugging his Stetson low on his forehead. "Okay. I'm on my way."

Call looked at José, who nodded, indicating he'd heard and understood the conversation, then strode toward the truck parked a hundred yards away.

What had come special delivery? Call wondered. Well, there was only one way to find out.

Call entered the house through the back door and found Lupe waiting for him in the kitchen.

"So slow you are to get here," she said, with a click of her tongue.

"No, ma'am," he said, smiling at her. "I came split-lickety."

"Mmm," she said, glaring at him. "The special delivery is on your desk chair in your office. Go. Shoo. Get your tush from my kitchen."

"Hey, who taught you that stuff?"

"You. Now go," she said, flapping her hands at him.

Call chuckled as he left the kitchen, but a frown quickly replaced his smile.

What in the hell had come special delivery?

He entered his office, leaving the door open behind him, and strode across the room to look at the seat of his desk chair.

As he stopped, every muscle in his body tensed, and the sound of his thundering heart echoed in his ears.

Perched on the seat of the chair was Susie, Paige's bedraggled and much-loved cloth doll.

He reached for the doll, aware there was a tremor in his hand. As he picked it up, a soft voice floated through the air.

"It seems like a lifetime ago when I heard you talking to Susie as though she were a real person."

Call spun around.

And there she was. Haven.

In a pretty flowered dress, her hair a halo of golden curls, a tentative expression on her beautiful face, Haven was there.

Call couldn't move, speak or even think. He could only drink in the sight of her like a thirsty man.

Haven walked slowly forward and stopped three feet from where Call stood holding Susie.

"Call," she said, her voice not quite steady, "you told Susie she looked as though she'd been in a battle or two, or had been given a lot of hugs."

Haven glanced at the doll in his hand, then met his gaze again.

"We're like Susie, Call. We've been in battles, won some, lost some, but we survived. Then, when we found each other, we became the recipients of some mighty fine hugs."

"Haven..."

"Paige loves that doll, even though it's not perfect, shows signs of wear and tear. That's unconditional love, Call, the very best there is. And that is the kind of love I hold in my heart for you.

"These two weeks have been so bleak, so empty, so lonely. I was so hurt when you left me in Tux's care at the warehouse. I couldn't understand how you could just walk away after saying you loved me. But I've had time to sort it all through, and I realize that because you *do* love me very much, you felt you had to go so that Paige and I could return to our safe world.''

"Yes, because—"

"Please, Call, let me finish. I'm putting aside my pride to come here, but I had to because I love you more than I can even begin to tell you.

"My heart aches for you because of what happened to Cathy and David Call. I see now how you felt that history was repeating itself, that to be close to you meant being in a dangerous place.''

"That's true, Haven,'' he said, his voice gritty.

"Oh, no, my love, it isn't,'' she said, tears brimming her eyes. "That's all behind us now *if* you'll put it to rest, let the ghosts go, disappear. You can live in the past, or you can step into the now and the future...with me. My sunshine world is cold and empty without you. I love you. I need you. Please, Call? Will you share the tomorrows with me?''

Haven lifted one trembling hand and held it out, palm up.

Call waited for the onslaught of cruel voices to hammer against his mind, demand that he remember who he was, what he'd done, where he'd been and where he was sentenced to stay for the rest of his life.

But all was still.

A sense of peace washed over him; a warmth greater than the brightest Texas sun consumed him.

He had traveled far in the darkness, alone, but now he was home, in the sunshine, with Haven.

And he was filled with the greatest joy he had ever known.

"Call?" Haven whispered, as a sob caught in her throat. "Please?"

He set Susie gently on the desk, then placed his large hand in Haven's small, delicate one. In the next instant he drew her close, nestling her to him as he wrapped his arms around her and buried his face in her fragrant, silky curls.

"There you go," Haven said, smiling through her tears, "darlin'."

She encircled his waist with her arms and lifted her head to receive his kiss. As their lips met, the commitment to forever was made. The dark ghosts of danger and evil were flung into oblivion for all time.

There was only Haven and Call . . . and sunshine.

On the day of the wedding, Call rose at dawn, intent on accomplishing a special task before driving into Houston to repeat the vows that would make Haven his wife.

When he drove away from the Triple S toward the rest of his life, a pristine white picket fence surrounded the front of the house, a house that by day's end would become a home overflowing with love.

*   *   *   *   *

Take 4 bestselling love stories FREE

Plus get a FREE surprise gift!

Montana Mavericks™

Stories that capture living and loving beneath the Big Sky, where legends live on...and the mystery is just beginning.

Watch for the sizzling debut of
MONTANA MAVERICKS in August with

ROGUE STALLION

by Diana Palmer

A powerful tale of simmering desire and mystery!

"The powerful intensity of Diana Palmer's storyline is exceeded only by the sizzling tension between her protagonists." —*Affaire de Coeur*

And don't miss a minute of the loving as the mystery continues with many more of your favorite authors!

Only from **Silhouette®**

where passion lives.

MAVT

SILHOUETTE®

Desire®

Big Bad WOLFE

WOLFE WATCHING
by Joan Hohl

Undercover cop Eric Wolfe knew *everything* about divorcée Tina Kranas, from her bra size to her bedtime—without ever having spent the night with her! The lady was a suspect, and Eric had to keep a close eye on her. But since his binoculars were getting all steamed up from watching her, Eric knew it was time to start wooing her....

WOLFE WATCHING, Book 2 of Joan Hohl's devilishly sexy Big Bad Wolfe series, is coming your way in July...only from Silhouette Desire.

IT'S OUR 1000TH SILHOUETTE ROMANCE, AND WE'RE CELEBRATING!

JOIN US FOR A SPECIAL COLLECTION OF LOVE STORIES
BY AUTHORS YOU'VE LOVED FOR YEARS, AND
NEW FAVORITES YOU'VE JUST DISCOVERED.
JOIN THE CELEBRATION...

April
REGAN'S PRIDE by Diana Palmer
MARRY ME AGAIN by Suzanne Carey

May
THE BEST IS YET TO BE by Tracy Sinclair
CAUTION: BABY AHEAD by Marie Ferrarella

June
THE BACHELOR PRINCE by Debbie Macomber
A ROGUE'S HEART by Laurie Paige

July
IMPROMPTU BRIDE by Annette Broadrick
THE FORGOTTEN HUSBAND by Elizabeth August

SILHOUETTE ROMANCE...VIBRANT, FUN AND EMOTIONALLY
RICH! TAKE ANOTHER LOOK AT US! AND AS PART OF THE
CELEBRATION, READERS CAN RECEIVE A FREE GIFT!

YOU'LL FALL IN LOVE ALL OVER
AGAIN WITH
SILHOUETTE ROMANCE!

CEL1000

SILHOUETTE®

Desire®

Centerfold

They're sexy, they're determined, they're trouble with a capital *T*!

Meet six of the steamiest, most stubborn heroes you'd ever want to know, and learn *everything* about them....

August's *Man of the Month*, Quinn Donovan, in
FUSION by Cait London

Mr. Bad Timing, Dan Kingman, in
DREAMS AND SCHEMES by Merline Lovelace

Mr. Marriage-phobic, Connor Devlin, in
WHAT ARE FRIENDS FOR? by Naomi Horton

Mr. Sensible, Lucas McCall, in **HOT PROPERTY**
by Rita Rainville

Mr. Know-it-all, Thomas Kane, in **NIGHTFIRE**
by Barbara McCauley

Mr. Macho, Jake Powers, in **LOVE POWER**
by Susan Carroll

Look for them on the covers so you can see just how handsome and irresistible they are!

Coming in August only from Silhouette Desire!